Will tensed. "I'm not going to change, Bella."

"I know that. I don't want you to. And neither am I. All I want is a quick fling."

He frowned. His heart thumped. A quick fling? Was she for real? "No, you don't."

Bella let out a frustrated sigh and withdrew her hand to fold her arms over her chest. "I'm getting a bit fed up with people telling me what I want. Look, I've thought it through, at length, and I want an affair. With you. Assuming you're up for it, of course."

Oh, he was up for it. More than up for it. So up for it, in fact, that he was in agony.

An affair didn't have to hurt anyone, did it? Bella seemed to know what she wanted, and if she'd really thought it through as she claimed then he ought to respect that. She wasn't stupid; she was perfectly aware of what an affair with him would be about. As long as he kept his head, stuck to electrifying sex and avoided any kind of personal conversation, he'd be fine. They both would be.

"And then what?" he murmured as the possibility of an affair with Bella heated his blood and sent desire ricocheting around him.

"We go our separate ways." She tilted her head. "I haven't changed what I want," she said, "and I'm not going to. I still want to get married. I still want security and stability. However, in the absence of any progress on that front, I feel like some fun. Hot, t

Object? He could hard

LUCY KING spent her formative years lost in the world of Harlequin romance novels when she really ought to have been paying attention to her teachers. Up against sparkling heroines, gorgeous heroes and the magic of falling in love, trigonometry and absolute ablatives didn't stand a chance.

But as she couldn't live in a dream world forever, she eventually acquired a degree in languages and an eclectic collection of jobs. A stroll to the River Thames one Saturday morning led her to her very own hero. The minute she laid eyes on the hunky rower getting out of a boat, clad only in Lycra and carrying a three-meter oar as if it was a toothpick, she knew she'd met the man she was going to marry. Luckily the rower thought the same.

She will always be grateful to whatever it was that made her stop dithering and actually sit down to type Chapter One, because dreaming up her own sparkling heroines and gorgeous heroes is pretty much her idea of the perfect job.

Visit her at www.lucyking.net.

Other titles by Lucy King available in ebook

Harlequin Presents® Extra

SAY IT WITH DIAMONDS

LUCY KING

~ Just a Fling? ~

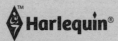

™ Harlequin®

TORONTO NEW YORK LONDON
AMSTERDAM PARIS SYDNEY HAMBURG
STOCKHOLM ATHENS TOKYO MILAN MADRID
PRAGUE WARSAW BUDAPEST AUCKLAND

Recycling programs
for this product may
not exist in your area.

ISBN-13: 978-0-373-52868-4

SAY IT WITH DIAMONDS

SAY IT WITH DIAMONDS

To Sophie, Robert and Dom—for help
with the details.

CHAPTER ONE

Bella, hon,
Alex has this friend he's been doing business with.
Single… Gorgeous… Clever… Loaded…. And he's really
up for meeting you. I know you're not keen on blind
dates, but I've met him and I think he'd be perfect for
you. So what do you say?
x Phoebe
PS—What are you doing for your birthday?

How long did it take to type *'Over my dead body'* and
'Burrowing beneath my duvet'? Bella wondered, re-reading
the email that had just landed in her in-box and glancing up
at the clock.

Seeing that she had ten minutes before her two o'clock
appointment was due, she swivelled back, shook her head in
bemusement, and hit the reply button.

What planet was Phoebe on? *Not keen on blind dates?* That
was the understatement of the century.

How could her so-called friend have forgotten the endless
nights they'd spent dissecting the disastrous blind dates Bella
had been on in the last six months or so?

How could Phoebe possibly have forgotten about the man
who'd showered spittle over her every time he opened his

mouth? The man who'd spent the entire evening addressing her cleavage? Or the man who, after insisting they go Dutch at a restaurant he'd invited her to, had got his calculator out to apportion the service charge?

Clearly Phoebe was so deliriously happy with Alex and so wrapped up in wedding plans that her memory had short-circuited.

Ignoring the sharp pang of envy at her friend's whirlwind romance and her subsequent state of bliss, Bella frowned. She was the first to admit she was eager to settle down—spending one's childhood trailing after a mother who'd had a racy, unstable, and, at one particularly low point, criminal past as well as a morbid fear of stagnating could do that to a woman—but she wasn't desperate. Or at least not *that* desperate.

And frankly, she thought tartly, if this friend of Alex's was as gorgeous, clever and as rich as Phoebe claimed, why was he still single? What was wrong with him?

As for celebrating her birthday, well, what was there to celebrate about *that*?

Once, when she'd been twenty-five, someone had asked her where she thought she'd be in ten years' time. She'd blithely replied, saying that on top of the multimillion-pound business, she'd have the husband, the family and the security she'd always longed for. She'd had no doubt whatsoever that it would happen.

But had it? No. Here she was, about to turn thirty-five and still single, without even a whiff of the boyfriend on the horizon, let alone the peal of wedding bells and the pitter patter of tiny feet. The last thing she wanted was to celebrate her failure on that front.

Bella resisted the urge to throw herself onto the floor and wail. Where had it all gone wrong? She was reasonably attractive. Interesting. Fun. And not entirely devoid of brain power. So why was she still sitting there, gathering dust, on an increasingly empty shelf?

It wasn't even as if she were particularly fussy. She didn't require a full head of hair or a six-pack in a husband. She didn't need fireworks and spectacular sex. She didn't demand five-star holidays or dinners in the finest restaurants the world had to offer.

All she wanted from a man was a desire to commit. To her. Well, that and an ability to keep bodily functions more or less under control, which possibly did narrow the field somewhat. But was a decent man *really* too much to ask for?

Bella sighed, planted her elbows on her desk and stuck her chin in her hands, and considered her position.

Maybe she *was* being too fussy. By the time you got to your mid-thirties, single, available men didn't exactly grow on trees. If you wanted one you had to grasp any opportunity that came your way, and following the recent spate of dating disasters, she had rather opted out of the game.

So perhaps it wasn't any wonder that what she'd longed for since she was a teenager was still nothing more than a distant dream.

Hmm. Maybe she ought to stop being so sceptical and give this friend of Alex's a chance. She didn't have a whole lot of other options, and how could one date hurt?

In fact, instead of mentally blasting Phoebe for setting up another blind date, she ought to be grateful that her friend hadn't yet given up on her. Positivity was the thing, she thought, sitting up and hauling her spirits up from where they were languishing somewhere around her feet. Because who knew? Friend of Alex might turn out to be The One.

Flexing her fingers, Bella typed a reply along the lines of *'Sounds great'* and *'Trying to forget about it'*, and hit the send button.

A split second later the sound of the buzzer ricocheted through her workshop.

Aha.

Abandoning the rest of her emails, Bella jumped to her feet. That would be her two p.m. appointment. Expecting an experienced jeweller and a valuation for a number items of jewellery, not a woeful woman with a penchant for self-pity.

Fixing a smile to her face and pulling her shoulders back, Bella sailed through the door into her shop. And stopped dead. Her heart thumped and the breath shot from her lungs.

Wow.

The man standing on the other side of the front door, cupping his hand to the glass and peering in, was nothing short of gorgeous. He was tall and dark and broad-shouldered. Wearing a navy overcoat open to reveal a pale blue jumper, a scarf and jeans, and sporting a tan that couldn't possibly be attributed to London in October.

Bella swallowed hard. When they'd spoken on the phone his voice had done the oddest things to her stomach, but she'd never imagined it would translate into real life. In her experience things rarely did. But William Cameron was just as attractive as his voice had promised.

And about her age, she thought, perking up considerably and automatically wondering whether he was single and available.

He straightened, gave her the barest glimmer of a smile as his eyes locked with hers, and Bella's mouth went dry. A strange kind of heat rippled along her veins. Her legs wobbled. Her stomach fluttered and then bubbled with excitement. Her entire body heated from the inside out and her bones began to melt.

He lifted his eyebrows enquiringly, gave her another half-smile, as if he knew exactly what was running through her mind, and pressed the buzzer again.

The sound brought Bella careering back to reality and she jumped. Blinked. And gave herself a quick shake.

Good one, Bella. That's the way to do business. Leave the client standing on the doorstep while you gawp at them. Very professional.

Ordering herself to get a grip and fervently hoping he wasn't a mind-reader, she walked over to the wide display table that sat in one corner of her shop.

And caught a glimpse of herself in the mirror that hung above it.

Oh, good Lord.

He wouldn't need to be a mind-reader to figure out what was going through her head. All he'd have to do was take one look at her face and he'd know. He probably already did. Because her cheeks were flushed and her eyes had darkened. Her breathing was erratic and her chest was heaving. Thank goodness the pattern on her dress disguised the rest of her body's reactions.

God, perhaps this was what was wrong with her, she thought, leaning down and pressing the button on the underside of the counter. Perhaps she was just too obvious. Perhaps she gave off desperate commitment-needy vibes or something. She stifled a shudder as she straightened. Heavens. If she did, how excruciating would *that* be?

It would probably be a good move to stop eyeing up every man she met as potential life-partner material, she told herself, taking a deep breath and plastering a smile to her face as he pushed the door open. Especially clients. However goodlooking.

Cool, aloof and polite was the thing. The consummate professional, in fact. How hard could it be?

Deepening her smile, Bella walked forwards. And then came to an abrupt stop. Her shop wasn't small by any stretch of the imagination, but the minute he set foot inside all the oxygen apparently whooshed out. Her breath caught in her throat, her heart lurched and all her blood rushed south, and for one horrible second she thought she was going down. Locking her knees and gulping in a shaky breath, she steadied herself and just hoped she'd managed to recover before he'd had the chance to notice.

Without the barrier of the door separating them, the overall impact of him was really quite startling. She couldn't work out which of her senses was most overwhelmed. Her vision when confronted with short straight hair the colour of obsidian, eyes as blue as iolite and the cheekbones that could have been chiselled from marble? Or her sense of smell when assaulted by the heady combination of sandalwood and spice?

As heat began to whip along her veins every inch of her itched to hurl itself at him to see if his body was as lean and muscled as it looked.

Oh, God. The man was not only gorgeous, he was practically magnetic.

So much for being cool, aloof and polite, thought Bella a little desperately as she fought to resist his pull. She was hot, bothered and feeling very rude indeed.

The door closed behind him and the lock automatically clicked into place. He tensed. Winced. And paled a fraction beneath his tan. For a split second she wondered why, but then he started running his gaze slowly over her, sliding down from her face to her breasts, her waist and then lower, and any curiosity she had vanished. As her body began to throb with awareness his lips curved into a faint smile, dragging her attention to his mouth, and all she could think about was what it might feel like on hers. *Wanting* it on hers. Hot and wet, hard and demanding.

The sudden thump of lust that walloped her in the stomach nearly knocked her off her feet and brought her slamming back to her senses. Bella blinked twice and battled for control. She really had to stop this. Yes, she wouldn't be averse to a relationship, and yes, she'd decided that she ought to grab any opportunity that came her way, but she drew the line at ravishing a client on the floor of her shop.

Belatedly reminding herself that she wasn't a teenager and she didn't throb, with anything, ever, she cleared her throat and lifted her chin. 'Good afternoon,' she said, holding out her hand. 'Bella Scott.'

'Will Cameron,' he said, wrapping his fingers around hers and giving her hand a firm shake before letting it go.

Two more of her senses hit the deck. His deep, wickedly lazy voice teased her ears, and her whole body tingled with the aftershocks of touching his hand.

The only sense left unaffected was that of taste, and that could be easily corrected. All she'd have to do would be to take one quick step towards him, reach up and plant a kiss on his mouth. Wind her arms round his neck, press herself against him, slide her tongue between his lips and she'd be able to find out exactly what he tasted like and exactly how hot, hard and demanding he was.

Agh, this was awful, she thought frantically fighting the instinct to swoon. It simply wouldn't do. Grappling for her elusive self-control, Bella drew in a deep steadying breath.

'Please,' she said, finally managing to get a grip and waving a hand in the direction of the chair on the other side of the table. 'Do sit down.'

Will folded himself into the chair and leaned back, taking up far too much space and, more disturbingly, far too much air. 'Thank you for agreeing to see me at such short notice.'

'Not a problem.'

As breathing, however, apparently *was* something of a problem, she wished that at the time she'd said she was too busy. Which she was. Ever since one of her necklaces had featured on the catwalk last year, Bella had had more work than she could really cope with. But the mesmerising tones of Will's voice over the phone had captivated her and the secret little longing to find out if the rest of him lived up to it had been impossible to resist.

'You mentioned you had some items to be valued?' she said, thinking that as it was way too late for regrets she'd better get on with it.

'I do.'

'For insurance?'

'Probate.'

'Oh,' she murmured. 'I'm sorry.'

He shrugged and his mouth twisted into what she presumed was supposed to resemble a smile. 'Just one of the many formalities to get through.'

Hmm. That wasn't quite what she'd meant, but his relationship with the deceased was none of her business. Or, to be honest, of nearly as much interest as what he'd brought her to value. She might have forged a career designing jewellery, but her first love would always lie with gemmology.

Bella's mouth watered as tiny thrills of anticipation began to course through her. 'May I see?'

He reached into his pocket, drew something from its depths and then leaned forwards and held it out to her.

She lowered her gaze and her breath hitched in her throat.

Oh, good Lord.

Catching her lip with her teeth, she took the ring from him, so mesmerised by its beauty that she barely noticed the tingles that rippled along her fingers when they brushed against his.

Utterly transfixed, she twisted the ring one way, then the other, and stifled a sigh of longing. She'd never seen anything quite so magnificent. The emerald-cut diamond solitaire was set in the platinum band and sparkled in the weak sun that had briefly broken through the heavy grey cloud of the autumnal afternoon and bathed the room. The stone had to be three carats at least. And flawless, judging by the perfect symmetry of the shards of light that were flashing all across the table.

'So what do you think?'

Yes, she thought as her heart twanged. Oh, yes. If—no, *when*—she got engaged she'd love something like this.

'It's beautiful,' she murmured, unable to stop the trace of wistfulness that crept into her voice.

'I couldn't care less what it looks like,' Will said flatly. 'I'm only interested in what it's worth.'

Bella jerked her eyes up to his and her little daydreamy bubble burst with a splat. What? How could anyone with an ounce of feeling in them be unmoved by such a beautiful thing?

Keeping her jaw firmly where it was instead of letting it drop in appal as it was threatening to do, she gave herself a quick shake. His attitude towards the ring was none of her business either, however much of a shame she thought it.

No. He was simply here for a valuation, not a lecture on gemmological appreciation. And from the tension currently radiating off him he was unlikely to welcome her opinions on the vast superiority of sentimental value over material worth.

Maybe he didn't have an ounce of feeling, she decided, picking up her loupe and holding it to her eye. Maybe he hated the stuff. Certainly something about the tight set of his jaw told her he wasn't the sentimental type. In fact he looked like the weary cynical type, and if that was the case he was definitely *not* her type, however gorgeous.

Firmly switching her attention to the ring, Bella turned it in her fingers. Examined it. Tilted it. Held it closer. Felt a stab of bewilderment and paused. Hmm. That was odd.

Perhaps there was something amiss with her loupe. Or her eyesight. Or maybe it was simply that with Will's gaze fixed on her as he watched her at work, her fingers felt as thick and as useless as sausages and her head felt as if it had been well and truly scrambled.

'Is something wrong?'

Very. On a number of levels. Lowering the loupe and hoping her concerns didn't show on her face, she glanced up at him. 'Would you mind if I did another test?'

'Be my guest.'

Bella rummaged around in the drawer for her touchstone and gently rubbed the ring against it. Then she added a drop of liquid and observed the results. Well, that was something to be thankful for, she supposed. 'Did you bring anything else for me to take a look at?'

He nodded, dug his hands into the pockets of his coat and spilled the contents on the table. As he did so his sleeves inched up and Bella's gaze instinctively dropped to his wrists. Her mouth dried. Tanned, strong and sprinkled with a smattering of fine dark hairs, they were completely mouth-watering. Up until now she'd never really thought a man's wrists particularly worthy of attention. Now they'd shot straight into the top five. Or at least Will's had.

Unable to help herself she slid her gaze to his hands and was instantly assaulted by the vision of those hands roaming all over her, exploring her, lingering and seeking, the long brown fingers delving and probing as they roused her. The vision was so vivid, so real, that Bella's temperature rocketed and her heart thundered.

Oh, this *really* had to stop. She'd never been so distracted. Certainly not when jewellery was in the picture. And right now, with the discovery she'd just made, she really couldn't afford to be.

Dredging up every ounce of concentration she possessed, Bella swallowed hard and turned her attention to the tangle of pieces piled on the table.

God, they were exquisite. And if genuine, worth a fortune.

'May I?' she said, casting a quick glance up at him.

'By all means.'

She picked up an art deco sapphire and diamond brooch and caught her breath. She put it back down and let a gold and emerald necklace slither through her fingers. Feeling like a child in a sweetshop, she felt her heart start pounding with anticipation. She'd never seen jewellery like it. Probably wouldn't ever again. If there was more where these pieces came from Will Cameron would have quite a collection.

Assuming of course that her suspicions didn't turn out to be correct.

As the excitement winding through her turned to trepidation Bella found a newer loupe in the drawer and braced herself to examine the rest.

Piece by piece, she performed the same tests. Taking her time as she scrutinised each item. Telling herself that she wanted to be sure, that she wasn't stalling.

But she was. Just a little. Because with every passing minute her heart sank a little further.

As she put the last piece back down Bella stifled a sigh. She didn't know who she was more disappointed for—herself for having had her illusions shattered or Will, who was only interested in the value of the objects and was, in all likelihood, going to be devastated.

'Well?' he said, arching an eyebrow.

'I'm afraid I can't give these a value,' she said cautiously. At least not the sort of value he was after.

'Why not?'

There was no way she could skirt around it. No way she could soften the blow. She could only hope that he wasn't the type of man to shoot the messenger.

Making herself look him in the eye, she took a deep breath and said, 'Because they're synthetic.'

CHAPTER TWO

Synthetic?

Will tensed. Impossible. They couldn't be. He must have misheard. Been distracted by the effect Bella appeared to be having on him or something. Because she was certainly distracting.

The minute he'd laid eyes on her, standing there stock still, staring at him from inside her shop, he'd clocked the long dark hair, the body poured into a clingy dress and the knee-high boots, and a shaft of awareness had shot through him making his gut tighten and his blood heat.

When she'd finally sprung into action and let him in, he'd fought back the nausea that always surged up inside him at the sound of a lock sliding into place by resolutely focusing his attention on something else. In this case, her.

Within a split second of running his gaze over her curves, the simmering awareness had turned to lust. Which had swelled to almost uncontrollable proportions when he'd spotted the flush hitting her cheeks and a reciprocal flame of desire flickering in the depths of her darkening eyes. He'd taken her hand, her scent enveloping him and vaporising his equilibrium, and had had to drum up every ounce of control he possessed not to haul her into his arms, push her back and spread her over the table.

Once he'd managed to rein in that oddly violent reaction,

he'd toyed with the idea of asking her out for dinner. God knew after spending the last couple of months sorting out his father's estate, he could have done with a bit of distraction and some light female company.

There was nothing particularly unusual about that. Will liked women; they liked him. He was currently single and he had no problem with affairs, as long as they remained hot and short. With his DNA anything else was out of the question.

No, what *was* unusual was that to his growing frustration it appeared that, while he still ached with raging desire, Bella had obliterated whatever spark of attraction she'd experienced, and had retreated behind an air of aloof detachment.

Which wasn't just unusual. It was baffling. And strangely disappointing, since he could barely remember the last time he'd had the opportunity to explore the heady delights of searing mutual attraction.

Not that he let it show, of course. No. He'd got used to arranging his face so that it didn't reveal what he was thinking or feeling years ago.

Perhaps a bit too well, Will thought, frowning and shifting in the chair. From the way her head was tilting and her eyebrows were creeping up, Bella was obviously waiting for some sort of response.

He rubbed a hand over his jaw and snapped his mind from perplexing women and evaporating dinner plans to the startling revelation that the samples he'd grabbed from the front of the safe and brought to be valued were synthetic.

How the hell could the stuff be synthetic? The collection had been built up over decades. Generations of his male ancestors had given the finest jewellery to their wives, and he was pretty sure that while virtually every single one of them had been lousy at keeping their marriage vows, they'd always bought the best.

Setting his jaw, he arched an eyebrow. 'Synthetic?' he echoed.

Bella nodded. 'The settings are real. The metal is genuine. And original. But the stones are paste.'

'Are you sure?'

'Pretty much. You see here?' She held up the engagement ring his father had given to his mother, and leaned forwards.

Will's initial instinct was to jerk back, but as that would imply he considered her some sort of threat—which was absurd—he held himself steady, even if it meant her proximity made his skin tighten and tingle.

Forcing himself to keep his eyes on the ring and well away from her mouth and the alluring way it moved, Will dragged his attention to what she was saying. 'The lustre is too dull and the light comes in at all the wrong angles. I'd need to double check, but I suspect the originals have been replaced with cubic zirconia.'

As her words sank in Will's blood chilled and he ruthlessly suppressed the mind-scrambling effect Bella seemed to have on him.

How on earth could this have happened? As far as he knew, the collection hadn't left the safe it was stored in for years. 'When?'

'It's impossible to say, but the settings look as if they've been manipulated recently. Probably within the past year or so.'

His jaw tightened and he sat back, making sure that his expression didn't reveal any hint of his thoughts. He might not care about the collection per se, or even the unforeseen plummet in its value, but he *did* care that the discovery that someone had been ransacking it had been made on his watch. He was its current custodian and it was therefore up to him to find out who and why and how far they'd gone. And then decide what he was going to do about it.

'I am sorry,' she said quietly, giving him a look full of sympathy he really didn't need.

Resisting the temptation to toss the whole lot in the bin, Will stuffed the jewellery back in his pockets. 'I trust your conclusions will remain confidential,' he said curtly.

Bella nodded. 'Of course.'

'Good. In that case, I'd like you to take a look at the rest of the collection.'

'There's more?'

Her eyes widened and sparkled, and Will's mind briefly went blank. Determinedly switching his focus to the dozens of boxes still in the vault and what might be lurking within them, he pushed his chair back and stood up. 'A lot more.'

'When?'

'Now?'

'I'll get my things.'

For someone who'd just been told that the ten items of jewellery in his possession were in fact worthless fakes, Will appeared remarkably sanguine, thought Bella as they purred through the streets of central London. If it had been her, she'd have been wailing from the rooftops and tearing her hair out.

Quite what reaction she *had* been expecting she wasn't sure, but it certainly hadn't been complete indifference.

However, the moment they'd climbed into his car—his chauffeur-driven blacked-out-windowed car, no less—Will had hauled out his smartphone and had remained glued to it practically ever since, issuing a barrage of instructions to a string of poor hapless souls on the other end of the line, only one of which appeared to relate to the rest of the jewellery he wanted her to check out. The vast majority apparently pertained to some kind of complicated share-dealing business, which no doubt accounted for the chauffeur-driven car, the cashmere coat and the six-figure watch he wore.

There'd been a brief hiatus when Will had switched from making calls to checking his emails, during which Bella, feeling she ought to make some sort of stab at conversation, had established that she'd been recommended to him by Phoebe's fiancé, Alex.

For one heart-stopping moment, it had struck her that Will might be the man Phoebe had been referring to in her email, but she'd dismissed the thought almost as soon as it had flitted into her head because Will Cameron did *not* strike her as the sort of man who went on blind dates.

Or the sort who delighted in small talk for that matter, judging by the monosyllabic way he'd answered her questions and had then effectively put an end to any more by resuming his calls.

Bella might have considered his absorption in his phone the height of bad manners if she hadn't been so relieved. Trying to control all the thoughts and emotions swirling around inside her was bad enough. Having to engage in any further conversation on top of all that—without ending up babbling like an idiot—might well have been one challenge too great.

Right now, it was a toss-up as to what was uppermost in her mind. The number one spot, she suspected, ought to be occupied by fascination with the outcome of her earlier investigations. In position number two should be anticipation at what she might find when she checked out the rest.

But she had the unsettling feeling that both fell way below the increasingly perplexing effect Will seemed to have on her.

When she'd leaned forwards earlier to explain what she'd discovered, she'd inadvertently found herself so close to him that she'd been able to make out tiny flecks of navy in the blue of his eyes. So close she'd been able to see a few fine silvery hairs at his temples and so close she'd felt the warmth of his breath on her hand. She'd had to imagine she was stapled to the chair to stop herself from leaping up and throwing herself across the table at him. Because her brain might be missing in action but she was pretty sure that that was *not* the kind of service he was after.

Now, within the confines of his car, she was even more spine-tinglingly aware of him. The enclosed space intensified his whole presence. His voice seemed to reach right down inside her and wind itself around her nerves. His legs stretched out a hands-width from her, and his taut energy made her shiver.

As much as she might wish otherwise, every hormone she possessed was sitting up and panting. Her eyes kept being drawn to the hard thighs encased in denim and her hands itched to reach out and touch him. Every now and then, when they went round a corner, his shoulder would brush against hers and she had to clamp her palms together and twist her fingers around each other to stop her from taking advantage and accidentally on purpose falling into his lap.

It really was most disconcerting. Made even more so by the knowledge that, while she was burning up with lust, Will couldn't be less affected by her. *He* certainly didn't seem to be suffering from any kind of distraction. Even when she thought she'd caught him checking out her legs, the expression on his face and the look in his eyes had been utterly unfathomable, which was annoyingly unflattering.

By the time the car finally drew to a halt somewhere in the depths of the City Bella was in such a state that when the chauffeur materialised at the passenger door to open it, she nearly tumbled onto the pavement in her haste to escape.

Teetering on her heels and grabbing onto the door for support, she gulped in great breaths of fresh air and cast a shaky smile of thanks in the direction of Will's driver.

Really, anyone would think she'd never experienced attraction before. Never felt desire. And she had. Loads of times. Not quite as mind-blowing or as instantaneous as this, but still.

Summoning strength to her legs, Bella released her vice-like grip on the car door, drew her shoulders back and tightened her grip on her equipment case and her wits. With superhuman effort she pushed Will Cameron's disturbing effect on her from her mind, and reminded herself that she was nearly thirty-five, sensible and mature, and it was high time she started acting like it.

A bank, she thought, glancing up. That was where they were. Not that it was like any bank she'd ever ventured into. No. No high street logo or hole-in-the-wall for *this* bank. Only a discreet gold plaque screwed to the wall and a front door that was right this second sweeping open to reveal an opulent hallway and a middle-aged man wearing a morning suit and a polite smile.

'Good afternoon, Your Grace,' he said, with the hint of a bow.

'Good afternoon, Watson,' said Will, putting a hand on the small of Bella's back and propelling her forward.

Bella's heart stuttered and she nearly tripped over the doorstep, startled as much by the form of address as by the feel of Will's hand on her back.

Your Grace? A bow? Who exactly was this Will Cameron with his chauffeur-driven car, his jewellery collection, his title and a bank that knew him by name? And how was it possible that her skin could burn beneath his hand despite the several layers of clothing between them?

'Is everything ready?' said Will.

Watson inclined his head. 'As you requested, sir.'

'Excellent. Thank you.'

'If you'd like to follow me?'

'You're a duke?' Bella muttered, just about managing to

stay upright as Will manoeuvred her along the corridor in Watson's wake.

Will nodded. 'I am.'

'Wow. I've never met a duke before.' At least not a real one. There had been that friend of her mother's, but he only claimed to be a duke on the Saturdays he gatecrashed various social events across the country and tried to persuade people to part with their fortunes.

'There aren't that many of us. But it's no big deal.'

Not to him, maybe, but then he wasn't the one who was wondering if he oughtn't to stop and curtsey. 'Rather young to be a duke, aren't you?' she murmured in the absence of knowing what else to say or do.

'The third Duke of Hawksley was eight months old when he took on the title. I'm thirty-six. Hardly young.'

But hardly the wizened old buffer she'd mentally plucked from the Dukes R Us casting agency either.

Bella frowned as something about the name niggled at the edges her brain. For some annoyingly out-of-reach reason it seemed familiar. 'Why didn't you say anything, Your—uh—Grace?'

'I didn't mention it because I prefer not to use the title,' he said, sounding as if he was gritting his teeth. 'And "Will" will do.'

Will will do what? Bella wondered, and then began to drown in the heat that flooded through her at the thought of exactly what she'd like him to do.

She'd like him to swerve off to the left, drag her down some dusty deserted corridor and back her up against a wall. She'd like him to lift her up, wrap her legs around his waist and crush his mouth down on hers. She'd like him to run his hands all over her and drive her mindless with need. Most of all she'd like him hot and hard and deep inside her.

At the bolt of desire that thumped her in the stomach Bella

went dizzy and stumbled. Would have hit the floor had Will not caught her arm and steadied her.

'Are you all right?'

Bella dragged in a breath and blinked a couple of times as she fought to wipe her head of the images. Oh, good Lord. She was fantasising. About Will. A *duke*. So much for thinking she didn't go for the cynical weary type, she thought dolefully. And so much for sensible and mature.

Wishing she could give herself a good slap, she pulled herself together. She could stop fantasising right now. Because if she didn't, she could well find herself getting completely carried away and have them riding off into the sunset together before the day was out. Which, given his indifference to her, was as unlikely as it was inappropriate.

'I'm fine,' she said a little shakily, wriggling away from beneath his grip before she did something really unhinged like deliberately letting her knees collapse and falling into his arms. 'Absolutely fine. These heels weren't designed for this carpet, that's all.'

A pathetic excuse if ever there was one but it would have to do. And it did very well until Will slid his eyes right down her body to the heels she'd unfairly blamed for her stumble.

His gaze was so laser-like, so intense, that it felt as if her clothes were disintegrating in its wake, leaving her standing there in front of him completely naked. And then, at the thought of *that*, she went so hot and trembly she nearly stumbled all over again.

'I dare say they weren't,' he murmured, lifting his eyes to hers, thrusting his hands in the pockets of his jeans and then swivelling round and striding after the butler.

For a second Bella just stood there, staring at his retreating figure, her heart thudding as she wondered if she'd imagined the flare of desire she'd caught in his eyes.

Must have done, she decided firmly, dismissing the thought

as nonsense and springing forwards in an effort to catch him up. Will had shown no indication that he was attracted to her whatsoever, so why would he start now? It had probably been a trick of the light or something.

'So the jewellery comes with the title?' she said, eventually drawing up at his side and trying not to pant at the sudden physical exertion.

'It does.'

And just like that a light bulb switched on in her head.

Oh, my.

Her brain spun and her heart raced. No wonder the name had sounded familiar. No wonder something about the samples he'd brought her had niggled away at her brain. And no wonder the collection was stored at one of the most prestigious private banks in the world.

Will was taking her to see none other than the Hawksley Collection.

Bella caught her breath as excitement ripped through her. The Hawksley Collection was a legend. The greatest, most romantic jewellery collection in the world. It consisted of around two hundred love tokens, gifts of eternal adoration and appreciation, bestowed by the men in the Hawksley family on the women they loved.

She'd heard about it, of course. Had read about it. Had secretly envied it and yearned for someone to love her with that much passion, that much devotion. But she'd never seen it. No one had recently. It hadn't been on display for years, which had only added to its glamorous mystique.

It was so achingly romantic. So completely heart-fluttering. So dreamily sigh-inducing.

And it was *fake*?

Questions clamoured at her brain. How? Why? Who else knew? And what would she find when she examined the rest? Would the whole lot turn out to be fake?

Her throat burned, her vision blurred and her mind boggled. Even if she could untangle the questions ricocheting around her head she could hardly ask. Not with the butler melting away and the security guard stepping forward to usher them into the lift.

'You go on down,' said Will, tilting his head in the direction of the lift, and backing away. 'I'll be with you in a couple of minutes. I have to make a quick call.'

Bella frowned. Another one? What could possibly be more urgent than *this*? This was staggering. This was humongous. But it was his collection, and if he wanted to let her go down ahead of him and leave her alone with the jewellery, who was she to argue?

'OK,' she said, trying to remain cool, which was almost impossible with all the emotions thundering through her. 'I'll see you down there.'

Will watched the lift doors close, shoved his hands through his hair and, abandoning all pretence of making a phone call, headed towards the stairs.

If he'd had *any* idea of the torture a half-hour car ride with Bella would induce, he'd have ditched the car and insisted on making the journey from Notting Hill to the City by Tube.

If they'd taken the Tube, he thought grimly, attacking the stairs two at a time, he wouldn't have had to spend the last thirty minutes struggling to keep his hands to himself. He'd have had plenty to concentrate on. Adverts. Announcements. Maps. Other people.

And yes, given his irritatingly ingrained problem with places and situations from which he couldn't escape, it would have been hell, but no more so than what he'd just been through.

Despite trying to keep himself busy with his smartphone, he'd had little else to concentrate on but Bella. With her dress constantly riding up and giving him an eyeful of slim thigh, and her scent winding into his head and making him think of hot exotic nights, Will's imagination had gone into overdrive.

It had had her giving him a smouldering smile, shooting him a come-hither glance and sliding across the leather towards him. As his body had responded with annoying predictability, his imagination had then got really carried away, and before he could rein it in Bella was bunching up her dress and sitting astride him, leaning down and whispering in his ear. She was arching her back, thrusting her breasts forwards, and then she was lowering her lips to his, sliding her tongue into his mouth and kissing him slowly, languidly, mind-blowingly as she writhed against him.

God, just remembering it now made him stiffen and ache.

Heaven only knew what instructions he'd given his team. He could have lost millions for all he knew. But it was either that or reaching forwards and pressing the button that raised the partition between the back seat and Bob, and setting about making his fantasies a reality. Which, based on the froideur with which Bella had treated him to date, he doubted would have been welcome.

She really did do chilly hauteur exceptionally well, he thought, scowling down at the stairs as the rigid way she'd held herself in the car popped into his head. She'd spent virtually the whole journey staring out of the window, hands clasped tightly in her lap, so tense and still that every time they went over a bump he wondered if she might shatter.

Although, actually, now that he thought about it, there hadn't been much chilly hauteur about the way she'd scrambled from the car, had there? Nor in the way she'd jumped when he put his hand on her back. And there very definitely hadn't been any chilly hauteur in the hot hungry look in her eye when she'd stumbled a few minutes ago and he'd caught her.

Will jerked to a halt and stood frozen to the spot, his brain racing as his pulse leapt and his blood heated.

Good God.

Maybe Bella wasn't quite as cool and aloof as she'd like him to think. Maybe he *did* affect her. Maybe she was as attracted to him as he was to her, and the icy distance she fought to maintain was simply her way of dealing with it.

And if that *was* the case, he thought, his spirits soaring as he leapt down the last couple of stairs and strode along the passage towards the vault, then he really *really* wanted to be around when all that latent smouldering heat erupted.

In fact, maybe, just maybe, dinner wasn't out of the question after all.

CHAPTER THREE

'THAT'S it. I'm done.'

At the sound of Bella's voice Will snapped his head up to find her rolling her shoulders and rubbing the back of her neck.

It had been three hours since he'd joined her in the vault and in those three hours these were the first words she'd uttered, at least to him.

By the time he'd caught up with her, she'd already got to work, so engrossed in taking her tools out of her case and setting her things up that she'd barely acknowledged his arrival. She'd cast a quick wide-eyed glance at the dozens of boxes neatly lined up on the table and had muttered that if she was to finish this side of midnight she'd better get on with it.

Will had figured that, as conversation didn't appear welcome, an invitation to dinner would most likely be ignored, so had planted himself at the other end of the table and opened up his laptop.

His plan had been to bide his time until a suitable moment to ask her out cropped up by clarifying any misunderstandings that might have arisen from his phone calls in the car, and catching up on some work.

Ha. What a waste of energy that had been. He didn't think he'd ever had a less productive three hours. Every time he tried to concentrate his gaze would slide over to Bella and

he'd find himself wondering exactly what colour her hair an
eyes were. Somehow dark brown and light brown didn't qui
cover it.

At one point she'd been examining a long multi-strande
pearl necklace, and he'd had a sudden vision of her lying o
the table completely naked, except for the pearls, with on
leg bent and an enticing smile curving her lips. His body ha
responded with a startling intensity and even now, an hou
later, he could feel a lingering ache behind the buttons of hi
jeans.

Not that she'd been aware of his musings, of course. O
his reaction to her. No. Her complete and utter focus on he
work was as fascinating and as impressive as his wasn't.

Shutting down the spreadsheet he'd spent the last hour sta
ing pointlessly at, Will closed his laptop. 'And?' he asked.

'The pieces on this side,' Bella said, indicating the grou
of boxes on the table to her left, 'are genuine. These,' she sai
turning her attention to the group on the other side, 'are not

Well, that was something to be grateful for, he suppose
The group on the right was a tenth of the size of that on th
left. 'Not quite as bad as I'd feared.'

Bella nodded. 'I agree. It seems that all the big stones ar
genuine. It's the smaller ones that have been tampered with
She frowned. 'Which does make some kind of sense, I guess

'Really?' None of it made any sense to him.

'Absolutely.'

'How?'

'Smaller stones are easier to replace. Fewer questions aske
when taken to be sold.'

'You think they've been sold?'

Her eyes jerked to his. 'Don't you?'

He didn't have a clue what to think. 'It's certainly a pos
sibility.'

'Well, I can't think why else anyone would do something like this. Do you have any idea who it could be?'

Will frowned. As far as he knew only he and his aunt now had access to the safe and for the life of him he couldn't see her raiding the contents. And as for his father, well, he'd been difficult, yes, but he'd never replace the stone in the engagement ring he'd given to Will's mother, whom he'd loved in his own warped way.

Nevertheless, he thought, cutting that avenue of thought off before he got tangled up in the memories and the guilt, *someone* was responsible. 'Not yet,' he said grimly. 'But I will.'

She tilted her head and the look in her eye turned quizzical. 'Is any of it yours?'

Will went still and felt some of the heat leave his body. 'On my father's death three months ago it all became mine.'

She flashed him a wide smile. 'You know what I mean.'

He did, and his temperature dropped a little more. 'I take it you recognise the collection.'

'I doubt there's anyone in my industry who wouldn't. The famous Hawksley Collection.' She grinned. 'It's legendary. So wonderfully romantic. The kind of thing little girls' dreams are made of.'

The kind of things *her* dreams were made of? he wondered darkly, catching the trace of wistfulness in her voice and feeling something hard and cold lodge in the pit of his stomach.

Romantic? What a joke.

Bella and little girls, and the rest of the world for that matter, might like to believe that the famous Hawksley Collection consisted of two hundred tokens of undying love, but what Bella, the little girls and the world didn't know, what no one outside the immediate family knew, was that his ancestors were a bunch of adulterous lying cheats, and that ninety per cent of the items in the collection represented an apology for one infidelity after the other.

'So?'

Biting back the urge to snap that it was none of her business, Will schooled his features and forced himself to remain calm. 'No,' he said flatly. 'In that respect none of it's mine.'

But it was hard to stay calm when all of a sudden his stomach was churning and his head was pounding.

It was hard to stay calm when he knew that the collection was built on a pack of lies and that the legendary status it had acquired was completely undeserved.

It was even harder to stay calm when he had to live with the constant knowledge that he ought to have contributed to that ninety per cent. Just once.

Before he had time to brace himself, memories of Tania slammed into his head and a steel band tightened around his chest crushing the breath from his lungs.

As clearly as if it had happened yesterday, he could see the look of devastation on his ex-girlfriend's face when, racked with guilt, he'd admitted he'd been unfaithful. He could still remember the tears, the recriminations, the pain he'd caused. And he was still, years later, plagued by guilt, despite her subsequent forgiveness and her acknowledgement that he hadn't been wholly to blame.

'Maybe you simply haven't met the right woman yet.'

Setting his jaw and pushing the memories aside, Will dragged himself out of the past. Not met the right woman? His gut twisted. With any luck he never would. Because there'd be no relationships for him. Ever. No marriage. No children. No family. No danger of wrecking any more lives, the way his ancestors had. The way he had. He simply couldn't risk it.

'Maybe not,' he said coolly, ruthlessly obliterating the pang of regret that jabbed at his soul and pulling himself together.

'Anyway,' said Bella as she pushed her chair back and stood up, 'what are you going to do?'

Good question. 'Put it all back in the safe while I decide,' he said, wishing that the whole damn collection could be forgotten about.

She sighed and began packing her kit away. 'It's such a shame,' she said, shaking her head a little. 'Practically criminal.'

There it was again, he thought, his attention zooming in on her face as much as her voice. The wistfulness. The longing. The hope. The same things he'd seen and heard when he'd first handed her his mother's ring, and had chosen to ignore.

But he couldn't ignore it any longer.

It was blindingly obvious to anyone who bothered to take a look that Bella was a romantic. She designed jewellery for a living and, according to Alex, specialised in engagement rings. Which meant she believed in for ever. As he very definitely couldn't believe in for ever, whether he wanted to or not, Bella was out of bounds.

Up until now, Will had obviously been blind. Bamboozled by unusually intense chemistry and at the complete mercy of certain parts of his body. Well, not any more, he thought, rubbing a hand over his face and watching her zip up her case. Now he was looking. And coming to the depressing realisation that all that latent heat bubbling inside her would have to be tapped by someone else, because he never got involved with women who wanted more than he'd ever be able to give.

Ignoring the stab of disappointment that struck him in the chest, Will stifled a sigh and got to his feet. He stalked round the table, plucked her coat off the back of her chair, held it open for her and squared his jaw.

His mind was made up.

Regret was pointless.

They were done.

* * *

So that was that, thought Bella, sliding her arms into the sleeves of her coat and forcing herself not to shiver when Will's fingers brushed the back of her neck. Watching him march back to gather up his laptop, she freed her hair from the collar of her coat and gave it, and herself, a quick shake.

And why wouldn't it be? Their business was concluded, and no doubt he had other pressing things to be getting on with. She certainly did.

Fastening the buttons, Bella stamped down on the disappointment darting through her and told herself not to be so ridiculous. She had no reason to feel as deflated as a month-old balloon by the knowledge that Will didn't want to prolong their encounter, like by suggesting dinner or something. Just because it was that time of day and she had been working flat out on his behalf all afternoon he was under no obligation to feed her, was he?

No. And even if he were, she reminded herself as she knotted the belt, she'd have declined, wouldn't she?

Because the way Will had clammed up and gone all tense when she'd tentatively probed him about whether any of the jewellery was his told her that he had issues, and while she might be in the market for a man—and was perfectly well aware that no one got to her age without some kind of baggage—on balance she'd prefer one without *too* much. Will, she sensed, had trolleyfuls of the stuff.

'Right,' she said, picking up her case and flashing him a cool little smile. 'Well, I'll be off, then.'

'Be sure to send me your bill,' he said, looking and sounding as if he'd already left, in spirit if not in body.

'I will.' She nodded. 'Email or post?'

Will shrugged. 'I don't mind. Whichever you—'

But whatever he had been going to say—and 'prefer' seemed probable—remained unsaid because he tailed off,

is gaze sliding away from hers and fixing on something
ver her shoulder.

Intrigued by the taut stillness that had gripped his broad
rame and the tightening of his jaw, she turned. To see a
voman hovering at the gate of the vault.

How old she was Bella couldn't tell. Her forehead was sus-
·iciously wrinkle-free and her hands were encased in gloves.
Her blonde hair was swept up and diamonds twinkled in her
ar lobes. Wrapped in a cream knee-length coat and shod in
·eautiful brown crocodile-skin heels, she had a timeless el-
·gance that Bella couldn't help but envy.

Whoever she was, however, Bella guessed that she hadn't
·een expecting company, not if the way her face was paling
nd her mouth was opening was any indication. In fact, Bella
vas pretty sure that had they been able to her eyes would be
videning and her eyebrows would be shooting up.

But before she could analyse the woman's facial move-
nents—or lack of—any further, she'd regained her compo-
·ure and glided into the vault.

'Will,' she said, lifting her chin and bestowing a regal
·mile on each of them in turn.

Bella glanced at Will, whose expression was as unread-
·ble as the blonde's, although she imagined for entirely dif-
·erent reasons. 'Caroline,' he said. 'This is a surprise.'

His voice was agreeable enough, but Bella thought she
·ould detect a hint of steel, and her stomach fluttered with
·omething that felt strangely like a thrill.

'It is,' said Caroline, clasping her hands together. 'I—ah—
·idn't expect to see you here.'

'Likewise.' He crossed his arms over his formidable chest
·nd stood there staring at her, as hard and unyielding as gran-
·te, and an involuntary shiver raced down Bella's spine.

'I thought you said you had business to attend to today.'

'I did.'

Bella stared at both of them, curiosity stabbing at her brain. Who exactly was this and what was going on?

'So what are you doing here?' asked Caroline.

'Checking up on my assets.'

A flicker of apprehension leapt in her eyes and then vanished. 'Really?' she said with a demure nonchalance that Bella had to admire.

'Really.' Will nodded, but didn't take his gaze off her and Bella was glad she wasn't on the receiving end of that stare. For despite her best efforts to remain cool and unperturbed, the poor woman was beginning to look as if she were being skewered to the spot. Having spent the entire afternoon in Will's disturbing company, Bella rather knew how she felt.

'And what are *you* doing here?' he said.

Evidently something she shouldn't be, thought Bella, what with all the tension and the undercurrents flowing around the place. It was becoming pretty obvious who was responsible for tampering with the jewellery, and if *she'd* been in Caroline's shoes, she'd have gone white and then bright red, mumbled something about just being passing and then dashed off.

Caroline, however, was clearly made of sterner stuff. She merely waved a vague hand and smiled. 'Oh, you know,' she said airily. 'Just popping in to take a quick look. I thought I might borrow something for the—ah—charity gala I'm attending tomorrow night.'

'I see.' Will nodded and for one brief moment Bella thought he was going to leave it at that.

As did Caroline, judging by the way her shoulders relaxed a little. 'So please don't let me keep you.'

'You aren't.' Will paused. Ran his hand along his jaw as if in deep thought and then said in a voice that was dangerously low and icily controlled, 'By the way, this is Bella. Bella's a jeweller.'

'How absolutely fascinating,' murmured Caroline, sounding as if she thought it was quite the opposite, but darting a quick smile in Bella's direction nevertheless.

'It has been. She's been valuing the collection…' He tilted his head but didn't take his eyes off her. 'She's been carrying out checks and tests and all kinds of other things.'

In the long seconds of silence that followed, during which horrified realisation gradually dawned in Caroline's eyes and the blood drained from her face, Bella couldn't help feeling another flash of sympathy.

'Ah,' the blonde murmured eventually. 'I see.' There was another tension-laden pause. 'Good at her job, is she?'

'The best.' Will unfolded his arms and took a step forwards. 'Caroline,' he said in a voice that brooked no argument and made Bella tingle in a highly disconcerting fashion, 'I think we need to have a chat.'

Caroline blinked. Probably would have frowned had her forehead allowed. 'Do we?'

Will stopped nodded. 'We do.'

'Well, if you absolutely insist, Will,' she said, lifting her chin and flashing him a tight smile. 'But perhaps later.' She glanced at her watch. 'I'm in a terrible hurry.'

'Now.' The word cracked through the air like a whip, and Bella jumped. Oh, this showdown was going to be explosive, she thought with a shuddery little thrill.

'Ah,' said Caroline, glancing over her shoulder and edging back towards the entrance to the vault. 'Well, now *really* isn't all that convenient.'

'Too bad,' he snapped.

And barely before Bella could figure out what was going on, Will was springing forwards, gripping Caroline's elbow and marching her out of the vault, leaving Bella standing there, open-mouthed in astonishment as she watched them disappear down the corridor.

CHAPTER FOUR

WELL, that had to be one of the oddest conversations he'd ever had, thought Will, climbing into his car twenty minutes later and slamming the door.

Once he'd got her alone, Caroline had had no option but to tell him everything he wanted to know. He hadn't even had to push all that hard; she might have started reluctantly, but once she'd got into her stride she hadn't been able to stop. In fact, the more she'd talked, the more Will had had the impression she'd actually found it something of a relief to be able to unburden herself.

Nevertheless, the ease with which she poured it all out didn't make what she'd had to say any less startling, or any less forgivable.

Will sank back against the leather and rubbed a hand over his face as his mind ran over his aunt's confession.

Apparently she'd been sneaking into the bank every week for the past six months, switching the jewellery one piece at a time.

Apparently she'd been bored.

And lonely.

Which, to be honest, had astounded him. As far as he'd been able to gather in the two months he'd been back, Caroline drifted from one social engagement to another, more often than not with a quick visit to her plastic surgeon in between.

If he'd taken the trouble to think about it he wouldn't have imagined she'd have had the time to be bored or lonely.

Or, for that matter, to become addicted to online bridge.

But she had. With a vengeance and a complete absence of talent.

At first she'd more or less broken even. But as the addiction had taken hold, her bank balance simply hadn't been able to keep up. Once her own funds had run out, she'd gone to the bank for a loan, and then, when her debts had begun to mount up, she'd hit upon the idea of selling the stones in the collection to both pay them off and facilitate her ongoing habit.

Stunned—because he hadn't known his aunt had even heard of the internet, let alone knew how to log on and embroil herself in the world of online gaming—Will had muttered that it was a good thing he'd flown back before she'd managed to get her hands on the Caravaggios. At which point Caroline had flashed her eyes at him and pointed out that caring for his cantankerous father hadn't exactly been a picnic, and he ought be grateful she hadn't sought refuge in alcohol or drugs or unsuitable men.

Swamped by an unwelcome and unexpected deluge of guilt at the realisation that by dashing off to the other side of the world he had left her to deal with his father's moodiness pretty much non-stop for the past thirteen years, Will had promised to clear her debts as soon as he got home, on the condition that she never logged on again.

With relief shining in her eyes, she'd thanked him, told him he was a good man, and scarpered.

The car pulled out into a gap in the traffic and Will closed his eyes briefly and pinched the bridge of his nose, his stomach churning as memories and guilt assailed him from all directions.

A good man?

Yeah, right.

He wasn't a good man. If he were a good man, he wouldn't have left his aunt to deal with his father by herself. He'd have stuck around instead of escaping everything by emigrating to the Cayman Islands.

If he were a good man he'd have swallowed back his bitterness and been on a plane the minute he'd heard his father was ill. He'd have come back for the funeral at least, instead of telling himself it wasn't a convenient time.

If he really were a good man he'd never have weakened and given in to a moment's temptation all those years ago.

At the very least he wouldn't have abandoned his manners for an entire afternoon.

The unfamiliar sense of shame that had spun through him when, moments before disappearing, his aunt had suggested he might want to go and see if Bella was all right jabbed him in the chest all over again.

Because as much as it annoyed him, actually Caroline had had a point. He really shouldn't have stormed out and left her standing there, undoubtedly thinking him arrogant and cursing him to heaven and back.

And she'd be perfectly justified to do exactly that on both fronts, because come to think of it, he reflected as he rubbed a hand over his face and sighed, none of his behaviour had been exactly exemplary this afternoon. After demanding she accompany him to the bank he'd then spent the journey there ignoring her. And then she'd asked him about his possible contributions to the collection and he'd sat there brooding and tight-jawed as he charged off down a traumatic memory lane while all she'd been doing was expressing an interest.

Yes, he'd been disconcerted by the effect she had on him, and yes, he'd then been poleaxed by the appearance of his aunt at the bank, and what it had to mean, but that was no excuse for abandoning civility. He hadn't even thanked her for helping him out this afternoon.

No wonder by the time he'd made it back to the vault to apologise for dashing off quite so unthinkingly she'd vanished. If it had been him, he wouldn't have hung around either.

Inwardly cringing at his uncharacteristically callous behaviour, Will was struck once more by the need to remedy the situation and shot upright.

By now, he reasoned, frowning as he pulled his phone from the pocket of his coat, Bella would be on her way home, and who knew where that was? So all he could do was give her a call to apologise and thank her profusely for her help this afternoon, and hope she'd accept his grovelling.

And, with any luck, that would be that, he thought, his head beginning to ache as this afternoon's unexpected string of events ricocheted around his brain. His conscience would be clear, the weirdly distasteful notion that Bella might think him arrogant would be appeased, and today, thank heavens, would be over.

Scrolling through his list of contacts to find her number, Will glanced out of the window at the driving rain and hoped she'd managed to find a taxi, because frankly he didn't think his conscience could cope with the idea of her having to battle the weather on top of everything else.

And then out of the corner of his eye he caught the flash of fuchsia pink and as his stomach plummeted he realised she hadn't and it was going to have to.

Because there she was, striding along the pavement, holding her equipment case on her head, bending forwards against the rain, glowering at the ground and looking as if she was muttering to herself.

Narrowing his eyes as he watched her and feeling another stab of guilt attack his conscience, Will abandoned his phone and stuffed it back in his pocket. He couldn't ignore her. Not again. Not when he still owed her an apology.

Gritting his teeth, he leaned forward to tell Bob to slow down and pull over, because offering her a lift home was the least he could do.

It would have to be raining, wouldn't it? thought Bella glumly, trudging along the street to the nearest Tube stop and trying to avoid the puddles.

If only she'd brought her umbrella. If only she'd been wearing a mackintosh and wellies instead of a cashmere coat and brand-new suede boots. If only she'd been able to find a taxi. But free taxis in central London when it was pouring with rain were as rare as pink diamonds.

As, apparently, were manners in peers of the realm.

The wind flapped at the bottom of her coat, chilling her knees, and the indignation that had surged through her the minute she'd found herself alone in the vault flooded back.

How could Will have just left her there without so much as a 'thank you for your help' or a 'would you mind seeing yourself out?' How could he have forgotten about her quite so comprehensively the second something more interesting and important had come along? So clearly Caroline had been up to no good, and of course Will would have wanted to get to the bottom of it, but he could have said *something*.

But had he? No. Once she'd served her purpose he'd barely spared her a second thought. He'd simply marched off, Caroline in tow, on top of everything else depriving her of the showdown she'd been looking forward to.

Rain trickled down her collar and she swore beneath her breath. Huh. What exactly had he expected her to *do*? Hang round like some sort of minion until he deigned to come back? *If* he'd deigned to come back? Or hadn't she even crossed his mind?

She scowled down at the shiny wet pavement. It was so rude. And OK, so Will was a duke, but that didn't give him the right to dismiss lesser mortals with quite such ease.

But perhaps that was typical of someone like him, she thought darkly, hopping to one side to avoid a puddle the size of the Mediterranean as her mind ran over the events of the afternoon.

He hadn't exactly asked if she'd been free to accompany him to the bank, had he, the arrogant man? He'd just assumed. Commandeered her entire afternoon and then once he'd got what he wanted had unceremoniously ditched her.

At some point this afternoon she'd clearly lost her mind. Because what on earth had she been thinking, dropping everything she'd been planning on working on today and following Will like some kind of soppy smitten fool?

Usually she worked to a strict timetable. Usually she prioritised. Usually *she* never pushed things aside when something better came along. She liked to think she was more professional and better organised than that.

But what had she done this afternoon? Let herself be carried away by a very well-packaged man with an intriguing jewellery problem.

And to think that up until the point he'd stormed out, she'd actually been finding all that pent-up iciness, all that glowering and glinting and frowning, attractive. To think that Will had been exuding unyielding alpha maleness from every pore and she had been a hair's breadth away from swooning. God. She'd always believed she'd abhorred that kind of attitude, yet there she'd been, quivering with lust and wondering what it would be like to have all that passion directed at her. So what kind of a perverse idiot did that make her?

Catching sight of the Tube sign, Bella quickened her pace, her heart thumping wildly with every step.

And who was this Caroline woman with her frozen face

and fabulous wardrobe anyway? Will hadn't bothered to introduce them so for all Bella knew she could be his *wife*. Stumbling on a loose paving stone and accidentally planting her foot in a puddle, she felt water seep through to her toes and her resentment tripled.

Oh, she'd be sending him a bill all right, she thought, shivering as a chilly gust of wind slapped rain at her stinging cheeks. Make no mistake about that. In fact, she'd be charging him double. For the urgency of the job and the lack of notice he'd given her. And she'd also be adding extra for the damage done to her coat and boots. So that would probably triple the bill, but who cared? She doubted he'd even—

'Bella?'

The familiar deep voice cut through her thoughts and Bella jerked to an abrupt halt, her insides leaping all over the place as she blinked the rain from her eyes and swung round.

At the sight of the outrageously gorgeous, abominably rude and unfairly dry head sticking out of the window of the car that was purring alongside her, her heart, the treacherously pathetic organ it was, skipped a beat even as her indignation soared.

Oh, this was great. Just great. He would have to turn up *now*, wouldn't he, looking all cool and relaxed and sexy when she was doing an excellent impression of a drowned rat? An extremely cold, extremely stroppy drowned rat.

'What do you want?' she said, too fed up with everything to care that she was the one now sounding rude.

'Would you like a lift?'

Yes. 'No, thanks,' she said mutinously. 'I'm fine.'

'It's pouring.'

'I had noticed,' she said, aiming for withering but finding withering annoyingly hard to do when her hair was plastered to her face, her arms ached from trying to protect her head with her weighty equipment case and her feet squelched in her boots.

'So get in the car and I'll take you home.'

'I'm happy to take the Tube.' Bella sniffed and planted her feet a little deeper into the moral high ground. 'Besides I wouldn't want to put you to any more trouble.'

Good. That was better. This time she *had* managed to inject a trace of sarcasm into her voice, she thought with a surge of satisfaction. Not that it appeared to be having any effect on him whatsoever, judging by the blinding smile he flashed at her.

'You wouldn't be putting me to any trouble. In fact you'd be doing me a favour.'

Another one? 'How?' she said archly, even more irritated by the way her stomach flipped like a pancake at his smile.

'You'd be saving me a phone call.'

So now he was stingy as well as rude? Just as well she didn't want to have anything to do with him. 'Fabulous.'

The smile turned into a broad grin, as if he was perfectly aware of her mood and completely unfazed by it, and Bella scowled.

'I'd like to apologise for abandoning you at the bank like that,' he said smoothly. 'Preferably in the privacy of the car, although I'm perfectly happy to do it on the pavement if you really have something against accepting a lift.'

Oh. Bella blinked and stared at him, feeling herself begin to waver as her indignation receded a little both at the smile and the look of sincerity on his face.

Hmm. Right. Well. If he wanted to apologise, who was she to argue? It was the least she deserved. But as for making him do it on the pavement, well, while part of her quite wanted him to get the drenching she had, another part of her pointed out that if she kept on refusing to get into his car she'd sound like an idiot and Will would be perfectly justified in wondering if she wasn't protesting just a bit too much.

Besides she was soaking and shivering and the moral high ground was getting soggier by the second. The Tube would be steamy and crowded and horrible, and here she was being presented with a lovely warm, dry alternative.

There wasn't really any contest, she thought, lowering her case and dashing towards Will's car. She might have lost most of her mind this afternoon, but it hadn't yet gone completely.

'I'll ruin your upholstery,' she muttered as he opened the door, unashamedly wishing she were a whole lot wetter so she could really do some damage.

He ran his gaze over her and, dammit, if her body didn't burn at his slow leisurely perusal. 'Not a problem in the slightest,' he said with another of those devastatingly sexy grins. 'Fair's fair, after all.'

Five minutes later Will was beginning to wish that he'd never spotted Bella on the pavement. His intentions might have started out all chivalrous and noble, but they were rapidly galloping in entirely the opposite direction.

The surge of triumphant satisfaction that had shot through him when she'd finally given in and slid into the car had long since vanished beneath a heat and a need that he'd thought he'd eradicated.

Eradicated? Yeah, right. How he could have been so foolishly naïve to have thought *that* he had no idea. The minute she'd slammed the door and started peeling off her clothes every inch of him had leapt to attention, pulsating with an awareness that he couldn't ignore, however much he'd like to.

Bella's case sat on the floor of the car that up until now he'd always considered to be quite spacious. Next to it lay her boots, which she'd unzipped and eased off a moment ago revealing shapely ankles and slim calves. She'd wiggled her toes and sighed in the kind of satisfied way that had Will instantly imagining a dozen other scenarios in which she might be sighing in a satisfied way.

Now she was unknotting the belt of her coat and undoing the buttons and he had to curl his hands into fists to stop himself reaching out and helping her. Every movement she made sent a waft of her scent up his nostrils and frazzled his brain. She ran her fingers through her hair and shook her head back a little and it made him think of hot steamy showers and slick wet skin.

As she twisted her hair into a thick dark rope her elbow briefly brushed against his shoulder and for one sizzling moment he thought he'd been electrocuted. His entire body burned as if it had gone up in flames and his heart practically stopped.

Will stifled a groan and with mammoth effort switched his gaze to the shops sliding by. He might have decided he wasn't going to pursue Bella but his body, stiffening and tightening and aching all over, clearly hadn't got the message.

Gritting his teeth as he forced down the desire he really ought not to be feeling, he dragged his mind back to his original intentions and cleared his throat. 'I am sorry for leaving you alone like that,' he said, forcing himself to glance over at her. 'It was unforgivable. I don't know what came over me.'

Bella arched an eyebrow and flashed him a look that suggested she could think of a few things. 'Did you solve the mystery of who's been messing around with the jewellery?'

'I did.'

'And?'

'Turns out my aunt has a few…issues…but it's a long and not particularly exciting story,' he said, deliberately vaguely because, while he might be prepared to apologise for *his* failings, he hadn't lost his mind to the extent that he'd go into Caroline's.

Bella went still and stared at him, her eyes widening. In the dim light inside the car he could make out the raindrops that still clung to her eyelashes and the flush on her cheeks from the stinging wind and it made his pulse hammer, despite his efforts to stop it. 'Caroline is your aunt?'

Will nodded. 'My father's younger sister. Older than she looks. Why? Who did you think she was?'

'I had no idea,' said Bella frostily. 'You didn't introduce her.'

'No. I'm sorry about that too.'

She shot him a look that he felt right in the pit of his stomach, and then nodded briefly. 'Apologies accepted.'

And didn't that make him feel absurdly relieved?

'How long did you wait?' he muttered, wondering what it was about her in particular that got to him and why he was finding it so difficult to think straight.

'Longer than I should have,' she said, glaring at him for a second then folding her arms over her chest, crossing her legs and sitting back.

Will rubbed a hand along his jaw, rapidly coming to the conclusion that, contrary to his earlier self-assurances, at some point over the last ten minutes he *had* actually lost his mind. Up until now he'd never considered himself to be much of a masochist but now he thought he might have to reassess his opinion. Because Bella, with her flashing eyes and pouty mouth and general air of stroppiness, was seriously turning him on.

He glanced over at her and his blood heated. If it hadn't been such a cliché and if he hadn't thought she'd slap him, he'd have told her she looked beautiful when she was angry. And sexy.

And as for her mouth, he thought, his gaze dipping to it,

well, that was something else. His body tightened and his pulse hammered as the overwhelming need to know what it felt like, what it tasted like, spun through him.

'Where would you like me to drop you?' he said, his voice sounding strangely hoarse as he battled to bring his body under some sort of control.

'My shop would be fine,' she said coolly. 'I live above it.'

'How convenient.'

'It is.'

'How long have you had it?'

'Seven years.'

During which she'd made quite a name for herself, according to Alex who'd heard it from Phoebe. 'Bella Scott' was apparently *the* place to go if you wanted a unique and unusual piece of jewellery designed.

'What's Bella short for?' he asked in the vague hope that inane small talk might detract him from thinking about how unique and unusual she was and how much he'd like to haul her into his arms and kiss the life out of her.

'What?' She blinked and stared at him.

'Your name. What's it short for?'

She bristled. 'What does that have to do with anything?'

'I'm interested.'

She hmmed. Then lifted her chin and sniffed. 'Belladonna, if you must know.'

Will felt his eyebrows shoot up as a smile curved his mouth. 'Unusual.'

'Yes, well, unfortunately my mother has a long-standing obsession with homoeopathy.'

She didn't sound as if she thought much of that particular occupation and he fought back a grin. 'And actually remarkably apt.'

Bella frowned and glared at him. 'You think I'm deadly?'

she said, the tone of her voice leaving him in no doubt about what she thought of *that*.

'I think you're beautiful,' he said, wondering what on earth he was doing but finding it hard to care given the way his resolve was disintegrating beneath the overwhelming pressure of wanting her.

Her reaction to his words was unexpectedly dramatic, the change in her palpable. For a moment there was utter silence. Then she let out a shuddery little sigh, her whole body softening and Will felt the slow beat of desire start up inside him as he realised with relief that she wasn't going to slap him.

In fact he got the heady feeling that she was going to do the opposite. He watched her swallow hard, her eyes beginning to sparkle and gleam in the inky darkness of the car. He could feel the heat radiating off her body, caught the flicker of interest leaping in the depths of her eyes and heard the almost imperceptible quickening of her breathing. Her tongue darted out to wet her lips and his gaze lingered on her mouth, lust whipping along his veins and tiny fires igniting in the pit of his stomach.

The atmosphere in the back of the car instantly thickened and vibrated and Will couldn't resist any longer. 'Although you're pretty deadly too,' he added softly. 'You're certainly killing me.'

'Am I?'

'You know you are.'

'Sorry.'

'Really?'

'No.' A slow seductive smile spread across her face and Will's pulse raced at the hot knowing look that appeared in her eye.

So Bella wasn't fling material. So he shouldn't go there. But what was one kiss? One simple harmless little kiss. It wasn't as if he'd let things get out of control or anything. And

he was willing to bet everything he had that she longed to
know what it would feel like as much as he did.

With his head spinning and his heart pounding Will leaned
forward and pressed the button that connected the back of
the car to the front. 'Bob?'

'Yes, sir?' came the tinny voice.

'Back to where we came from, please. And take a circuitous route.'

As the partition separating them from Bob swished up Will
turned to her, every inch of his body straining with desire.

'I'm flattered you enjoy my company so much,' Bella said,
her voice sounding all husky and breathy as she stared at him.

Will reached out to take a lock of her hair and wound it
around his fingers. His knuckles brushed against her cheek
and he felt her shudder. 'Not just your company,' he murmured, tugging her slowly, irrevocably towards him.

CHAPTER FIVE

BELLA'S last coherent thought as Will's arm came round her and his head descended was that she was so out of her depth she might as well be sinking to the bottom of the Atlantic with lead weights attached to her ankles.

The minute she'd got into his dry warm car, his eyes had been on her every movement and any control she'd felt, any spurious inch of moral high ground she might have occupied, had vanished.

How she'd managed to peel off her sopping clothes with such shaking hands and trembling fingers she had no idea. When her elbow had accidentally brushed his shoulder she'd nearly leapt off the seat, so strong had been the electric charge that coursed through her body. The heat and attraction and need that had then gripped her had been so overwhelming, so alarming that she'd felt she had to cling onto her indignation as some kind of defence against him.

Ha. Defence? It was becoming pretty clear that she had absolutely no defence against Will. He'd told her he thought she was beautiful and that had been that. The last smidgeon of resentment still bouncing around inside her had evaporated and she'd crumbled.

Somewhere in the hazy fog of desire that had replaced her brain she was dimly aware that she was once more being skilfully manoeuvred. Not that her melting, quivering body seemed to care. No. One touch, and her fickle body decided that the more skilfully Will wanted to manoeuvre her, the better.

Bella stared at him, her mouth going dry and her heart beginning to gallop. Her breathing shallowed as if he'd stolen her oxygen and at his heat, his scent, his proximity and the intensity of the look in his eyes, her insides liquefied.

She held her breath as his head moved lower, closer. His scent engulfed her and she went dizzy. Her mouth actually watered. The slow steady beat of desire began to drum through her and something inside her melted.

She'd spent every second since she'd met him desperate to find out what he tasted like, and it had been driving her nuts. Frankly, she was through with guessing. And through with waiting.

It was only a kiss, after all, and how could one little kiss hurt? She'd had countless kisses and none of them had ever hurt. Why should this one be any different?

Bella parted her lips, felt their breaths mingle for a second and then she moved forwards and settled her mouth on his.

She felt him jolt. Tense a little, and she wondered if he'd jerk back. But he didn't, so she closed her eyes, ran her tongue along his lower lip, revelling in its firmness and heat, then slid inside.

And immediately lost all sense of reality.

Sensations cascaded through her as she gave up to the deliciousness of his mouth. Liquid fire replaced the blood in her veins. Pounding desire filled every cell of her body and her insides began to quiver.

Oh, God, Bella thought as their tongues tangled languidly. *Now* she knew what he tasted like. He tasted of excitement. Arousal. Wickedness. And she was utterly intoxicated.

Unable to prevent it, she sighed into his mouth and he responded instantly, moving the hand that wasn't caressing her hip to the nape of her neck, sliding his fingers through her hair and angling her head to deepen the kiss. And then he was back in control, claiming possession of her mouth, her lips, her senses.

She clutched at the back of the seat for support with one hand and curled the other into a fist, digging her nails into her palm in a desperate attempt to focus on something other than the desire clawing at her stomach. But at the devastation he was wreaking on her, at the mercy of such exquisite need, she didn't stand a chance. She groaned and leaned into him, and then Will was hauling her onto his lap, pulling her closer and anchoring her against him as he devoured her mouth.

Bella twisted slightly so that her torso was plastered against his, wrapped her arms around his neck and felt her mind go blank. All that existed was the two of them on the back seat of his car and the scorching heat they seemed to generate.

He broke away and slid his mouth along her jaw to her ear. 'This was just supposed to be a kiss,' he whispered raggedly.

'It still is.' And as long as it stayed that way she'd be fine.

'You think?' The warmth of his breath on her skin made tiny shivers scuttle all over her.

'Absolutely.'

'So stop me,' he muttered, tugging at the tie that secured her dress so that it loosened enough for him to slip a hand beneath the flimsy fabric to find her breast.

Bella gasped as his hand cupped her there and his thumb brushed over her nipple. 'In a minute.'

'In a minute you might not be able to,' he said, dropping a trail of searing kisses down her neck and over the slope of her chest. He pulled aside the lace of her bra and took her nipple in his mouth and Bella bit her lip as a million tiny electric shocks shot through her veins.

And it was all too much. The feel of his body hard against hers and the wet heat of his mouth devastating her senses. The sizzling of her skin from where he'd kissed it. The scent of him winding up her nose and the rocking motion of the car. The way he'd been utterly impervious to her stroppiness and the confident ease with which he'd been prepared to apologise. And the fact that despite all earlier appearances to the contrary he seemed to want her as much as she wanted him.

God, it was all much too much. She wanted him to touch her everywhere. Needed him to touch her everywhere. 'In a minute I might not want you to,' she said hoarsely, somewhere in the depths of her mind thinking she must be mad but too far gone to care.

And then as lust began to pound through her Bella gave up thinking and gave in to instinct. She threaded her fingers through his hair and dragged his head up. Their mouths met and a shower of sparks darted through her as his tongue delved between her parted lips and tangled with hers.

Her hips twitched and she tilted them closer. When she felt the hard length of his erection press into her she moaned and the kiss spiralled out of control in seconds. The back of the car filled with her breathy groans and Will's ragged pants and the sounds made her excitement rocket.

He put his hands on her knees and slid them beneath her coat, beneath her dress and up her thighs and Bella shivered.

Until he stopped, jerked back and muttered a low oath.

'What?' she said, pushing her hair back and dragging in a ragged breath.

'Stockings.'

'Is that a problem?'

'I didn't think of stockings,' he muttered.

'Huh?'

Colour slashed along his cheekbones. 'Nothing.'

Will made an aim for her mouth but she moved back out of reach and tilted her head. 'Tell me.' He might not have been thinking about stockings but he'd definitely been thinking about something else involving her in this kind of a scenario, and the knowledge unravelled what was left of her brain.

He gave her a smile that she could feel right in the marrow of her bones, while his fingers continued to create havoc on the bare flesh of her upper thighs. 'On the way to the bank I imagined you doing this.'

Bella's eyes widened. 'You did?'

'Mmm.'

'But you were on the phone.'

He arched an eyebrow. 'Why do you think I was on the phone?'

She blinked. He'd felt it too? Way back then? So she hadn't imagined that flicker of desire in his eye when she'd stumbled...

The realisation that he'd been thinking about this as much as she had made her brain start up again and absorb this revelation. Her pulse leapt. All relationships had to start somewhere, didn't they? And yes, maybe dinner, a date or two, was the conventional method, but where had conventionality got her? Higher up the shelf, that was where. Her heart began to hammer as a thrilling notion planted itself in her head and took root. She'd done demure and sensible, and she was *still* single so why not throw caution to the wind, locate her inner vixen and start with sex? She couldn't end up any worse off, could she?

'So you imagined me like this?' She arched her back and gazed down at him.

Will nodded, his eyes glazing over. 'I did.'

'What else was I doing?'

'Writhing,' he muttered. 'You were writhing.'

Writhing she could do. 'Like this?' she said, rotating her hips and rubbing her breasts against his chest.

'Exactly like that,' he said hoarsely.

'Anything else?'

'You don't want to know.'

'Maybe I do.' And, heaven help her, it was true. She was burning up. Everything inside her had melted into a boiling quivering mass of need and she couldn't back out now even if she'd wanted to.

'Are you sure?' Will's hand moved higher.

'Absolutely.' She bit her lip as a thought popped into her head. 'Bob?'

'Soundproofing.'

'Effective?'

'You can scream if you like and no one would hear you but me.'

Ignoring the little voice in her head that wondered how he knew a thing like that, Bella lowered her head and gave him what she hoped was a seductive smile. 'Make me.'

His body churning and aching with need, Will stared at Bella and wondered how he could have got her so wrong.

Someone who wanted the whole relationship works, the whole 'for ever' nightmare, would never sit astride a man she'd only just met, give him a smouldering smile and basically order him to ravish her, would she?

No, a woman with a long-term relationship on her mind would be scrambling for the door handle and tumbling out of the car in her haste to escape. And Bella definitely wasn't showing any signs of wanting to escape. Instead she'd ensnared him with her body, her scent and her devastating mouth until he'd begun to feel as if he was the one who was unable to escape.

And why would he want to? Bella was a woman who knew what she wanted and was clearly as much in favour of no-strings sex as he was.

So why was he bothering to analyse a hurdle that clearly didn't exist? Why was he contemplating his principles when he had a gorgeous sexy woman wriggling in his lap and inviting him to make her scream? Was he nuts?

Shutting down his brain, Will concentrated on the feel of her against him, the warmth of her skin beneath his fingers and the smouldering heat in her eyes.

He slid his hands higher up her thighs, felt her tremble, planted his hands on her bottom and pulled her tight against him. Catching her mouth with his, he swallowed her gasp of shocked delight and tilted his hips. He felt her moan into his mouth and moved one hand round to slip beneath her knickers. Her fingers locked themselves in his hair and she arched her back against him.

He could feel her heat, her need. She was so wet, so slippery, so ready for him, that he didn't think he could stand it much longer. When he slid a finger deep inside her she let out a muffled ragged groan. He felt her muscles clench around his finger and heard her catch her breath as his thumb found her clitoris.

He rubbed and stroked and she shuddered. She ground herself against him as their mouths fused, teeth clashing, the ache inside him becoming almost unbearable.

And then she was dragging her mouth from his, leaning over to rummage around in her handbag with one hand, and fumbling with his belt with the other.

'Women really are good at multitasking,' Will said hoarsely, trying to focus on something other than the way every one of his senses was filled with her.

'You're not doing too badly,' she muttered, shivering as she pulled a condom out of her bag and ripped it open with her teeth.

Having unbuckled his belt, she undid the buttons of his fly, slid her hand beneath his shorts and freed him. The touch of her fingers on him blew his mind and as she deftly rolled the

ondom onto him Will had to bite down hard on his tongue
o stop himself climaxing right then.

Staring into his eyes, she lifted her hips and as his fingers
lipped from her he pulled her knickers to one side and then
inally she lowered herself onto him, taking him in inch by
ncredible inch.

At the white hot lust that thundered through him, Will
et his jaw and fought for control. But then she was sink-
ng down hard, sighing and rocking back and forth, and he
hought—as much as he could think—that he'd never seen
nything so arousing. They were both still fully clothed yet
vere as tightly joined as it was possible to be.

Will tugged her head down to his and captured her mouth
vith his. His heart hammered as she whimpered and then
began kissing him back as fiercely as he was kissing her, and
t tight coil of heat began to build deep inside him.

She moved up and down him and as he met her increas-
ngly frantic thrusts his mind went blank. All he was aware
of was the agonisingly delicious tension gripping his muscles.

And then somewhere through the thick hot fog in his head,
e heard her cry out. He felt her tense, arch her back and then
hatter and convulse around him and he couldn't hold him-
elf back any longer. Pulling her down and thrusting up hard,
Vill buried himself as deep as he could and, with a groan
hat tore from his throat, hurtled into oblivion.

How long they stayed like that, with his arms around her
nd her head on his shoulder, Will had no idea. Was it seconds? Minutes? Hours? However long it was, it was long
enough for them to have pulled up outside her shop.

'We should do this again,' he muttered hoarsely, his hands
stroking up and down her thighs.

'I'd like that.'

'But properly. How about dinner?' he said, thinking that

dinner—with Bella for dessert—was once more a most ex
cellent idea.

She raised her head and gave him a wide satisfied smil
as she lifted herself off him, ran her hands through her hai
and fixed her clothing. 'Dinner would be nice,' she said, he
voice so gravelly and satiated that Will wanted to yank he
back down and make her fracture in his arms all over again

Silently cursing the fact that he'd promised Caroline he'
sort out the mess she'd got herself into this evening, Wil
shoved his hands through his hair and put himself back to
gether. 'Are you free on Saturday?'

'I probably shouldn't admit it but I do believe I am.'

'Then I'll pick you up at eight.'

'Great.'

Twisting round, she reached for the door handle. Unabl
to resist, Will pulled her back into his arms and slammed hi
mouth down on hers. The kiss barely lasted a second, but i
was so hot and hard and electric that when he broke it off h
was breathing as raggedly as she was and his heart was thun
dering. 'Goodnight,' he murmured, wondering how the hel
he was going to be able to wait until Saturday.

'Goodnight,' she said, flashing him a blinding smile be
fore opening the door and disappearing into the night.

Bella closed the door to her flat above her shop and sagge
against it, her legs no longer able to hold her up.

Had she really just done what she thought she'd just done

While her brain made a stab at railing against the idea tha
she'd had sex with someone she'd only just met, her body as
sured her that she most definitely had. And how. God, an
how.

She'd known sex with Will was going to be good, but she'
never imagined it was going to be that explosive. When she'
taken him inside her she'd nearly passed out with delirium

ll control had fled and she'd let her body do what it wanted
nd sweep her away with the flow. And what a fantastic idea
nat had been.

She'd never imagined it was going to be that addictive ei-
ner. But the minute she'd lifted herself off him, she'd wanted
o sink back down onto him and ask him to tell Bob to go
ound the block a few times. When Will had given her that
corching goodbye kiss, she'd had to dash off before she could
rab him by the lapels and drag him into her flat with her.

Even now, her body still tingling and twitching with the af-
ershocks of her orgasm, the pulse between her legs throbbed
nd ached, desperate for more of him. She'd never known
eed like it.

And now she had to wait two days before she'd be able
o satisfy the craving. Bella let out a tiny groan. Agh. Two
vhole days. Two whole nights. Forty-eight hours. How on
arth would she manage?

Summoning strength to her limbs, she hauled herself to
er feet and wandered into the kitchen, dazed and confused
y the heady way she was feeling.

Who exactly was this man who'd dazzled her, bewildered
er and had her throwing caution to the wind and thinking
bout sex to the exclusion of all else? she wondered, opening
he fridge and taking out a bottle of wine.

She pulled the cork out, plucked a wine glass from the
upboard and poured herself a healthy measure.

Phoebe would know, but she could hardly call her, could
he? Phoebe would want to know all the details of how they'd
net and how it had panned out, and Bella wasn't sure she
vas up to dissecting what had happened just yet. Besides,
hoebe would probably tell Alex, who would probably men-
on something to Will, and Bella certainly didn't want *him*
nowing she'd been asking about him.

And yes, she supposed she'd find out more about him

at dinner on Saturday, but frankly she couldn't wait unt
Saturday. She wanted to know now.

Setting her glass on the kitchen table, Bella sat down an
opened up her laptop.

Research, she told herself. That was all she was doing
A quick check. Just to see. All perfectly normal. A sensib
precaution in this day and age, actually, she assured hersel
taking a sip of wine, then tapping Will's name into the searc
engine and waiting for the results to pop up.

When they did, a nanosecond later, her eyes widened
Wow. Ten thousand entries. So much for wondering how sh
was going to occupy herself for the next two days.

Feeling an idiotic grin spreading across her face, Bell
clicked on the first link and began to read.

One hour, a bowl of vegetable soup and another glass of wir
later, Bella was no longer grinning.

Her research had started off so well. She'd found out tha
Will lived and worked in the Cayman Islands, which no doul
accounted for the tan.

She'd discovered he owned a vast estate over there an
liked to windsurf and scuba-dive, which no doubt accounte
for the lean muscled body.

She'd learned that he was some sort of genius with figure
and derivatives, and she'd had a crash course in day trading

She'd learned that his family could trace its roots back t
King John, and that even without the dukedom he was a bi
lionaire.

She'd learned his mother had died of a stroke when he wa
twenty-three, and he'd emigrated shortly afterwards.

And then she'd discovered something else. Something tha
had wiped the smile from her face and was the cause of th
disappointment crashing through her.

Will dated. A lot.

According to the articles she'd trawled through and the photos she'd pored over, he rarely saw the same woman more than half a dozen times. In one interview dating from only a month ago, he'd been asked whether he was on the lookout for a duchess and he'd said no. 'Emphatically' apparently. When the interviewer had mentioned the Hawksley Collection and asked about love he'd said he didn't believe in it.

Bella rubbed her eyes, pinched the bridge of her nose and sighed. Wasn't that typical?

Will Cameron might be hotter than the Sahara in summer and he might have given her the best orgasm of her life, but for whatever reason he was a commitment-phobe. And therefore no good for her whatsoever.

Resisting the urge to drown her sorrows in the rest of the bottle of wine, Bella got up and went in search of her phone. That little voice inside her head yelling, 'Who cares?' could protest all it liked. She wasn't listening. Because she'd had enough of Mr Right Now. She was looking for Mr Right and, despite her hopes to the contrary, Will Cameron was Mr Wrong In Every Way.

CHAPTER SIX

IF HE'D thought his conversation with his aunt at the bank had been odd, thought Will, sitting in the library at Hawksley House, nursing a glass of whisky and staring broodingly into the fire, it had been nothing compared to the way in which the rest of the day had turned out.

Today was, without exception, the strangest, most surreal day he'd ever experienced and he wasn't sure he wanted to experience a day like it ever again. He'd had enough mind-boggling revelations and gut-churning trips down memory lane to last a lifetime. And as for the tangled financial mess his aunt had created, well, that had taken hours to unravel. God only knew what sort of trouble she could have ended up in if he hadn't found out what she'd been up to.

Aware that his hand had tightened around the glass, Will set it on a side table before it shattered and rubbed a hand over his face.

And somewhere muddled up in it all there was Bella.

When he'd woken up this morning he'd never in a million years have imagined that she would have slammed into his life. But she had. Like a tornado, whipping around, lifting everything up, churning it around and then dropping it back down in a chaotic jumble. She'd been unexpected. Unbelievable. And as sexy as hell.

If his body weren't still throbbing with the after-effects of the mind-blowing interlude on the back seat of his car he'd never have believed it had happened. But the ever present image of her writhing on top of him, rocking back and forth, biting on her lip and moaning told him it had been all too real. He might not wish to experience a day like today ever again, but he had every intention of experiencing *her* again.

Will ground his teeth and tried to drag his aching body back under control.

How in God's name was he going to be able to wait until Saturday? In fact why *was* he waiting until Saturday? Why on earth wasn't he taking her out for dinner tomorrow? So he'd arranged to have a drink with Alex, but he could easily postpone it. He was pretty sure that Alex, himself totally besotted with his fiancée, would understand. There was no need to suffer this agony any longer than was necessary.

He levered himself to his feet to retrieve his phone from his desk where he'd emptied his pockets earlier and then stopped, frowned and fell back down, his blood turning to ice.

What on earth did he think he was doing?

Since when had he contemplated ditching a friend for a woman? And since when had he brought forward a date because he couldn't wait? Where had his self-control gone? And more disturbingly, where had the idea that he might be besotted with Bella come from? He couldn't be besotted with her. He'd only just met her. Besides he didn't get besotted. Ever.

Will let out a growl of frustration. He'd wait until Saturday because he had to. Because that was the plan. Because he wasn't besotted. And because he had gallons of self-control. Somewhere.

The sound of his mobile ringing jerked him out of his thoughts and he jumped to his feet and snatched it up before he could analyse the sharp stab of hope that it might be Alex cancelling. 'Hello?'

'Will?'

At the sound of Bella's voice on the other end of the line Will's pulse leapt and his blood began to simmer as the desire gripping his insides intensified.

Maybe she didn't want to wait either. Maybe she was as much at the mercy of this as he was. In fact, now he'd dealt with the havoc Caroline had wreaked on her finances, maybe he could invite her round right now. Or head over to hers. He wasn't fussy. Just weirdly desperate to see her again. 'Who else?' he said, reining in his raging libido and telling himself to cool it.

'Of course.' He could hear the smile in her voice and his stomach flipped.

'What can I do for you?' he said, and rather hoped she was going to tell him exactly what he could do for, and to, her.

He heard her take a deep breath. Imagined her running a hand through her hair. Imagined running *his* hands through it again and felt his pulse spike.

'I'm calling to cancel our date.'

And then it slowed right down. All the heat and desire dwindled away and Will went strangely cold. What? Why would she want to cancel their date? 'I see,' he said, thinking that actually he didn't see at all. She'd seemed pretty keen earlier, moments after she'd come apart in his arms. 'Any particular reason?' he added, aiming for a nonchalance he certainly didn't feel.

'I'm busy on Saturday.'

Hmm. Will threw himself into the chair behind the desk and picked up the crystal paperweight blinking at him in the firelight. That was annoying, but fair enough. Perhaps, like him, she hadn't been thinking all that clearly at the time. And they hadn't exactly whipped out their diaries to coordinate. 'Then another day,' he said.

'I don't think so.'

'Why not?'

'I just don't think it's going to work out.'

Unable to glare at her, Will glared at the paperweight. How the hell did she know that? She hadn't given it a chance. And what was there to work out anyway? The only thing they had to worry about was sexual compatibility, and there was absolutely no problem on that front.

At the memory of just how sexually compatible they were, a bolt of lust tore through him as sharp and jagged as lightning, and he dropped the paperweight. On his toe.

Wincing at the pain, Will scowled, bent down to pick it up and put it back on the desk.

'Are you all right?'

The concern tingeing her voice irritated him even more. 'Fine. Just great.' He ground his teeth. 'What makes you think it wouldn't work out?'

A pause. 'I just know.'

He went still as a thought flashed across his mind. 'Are you involved with someone else?'

'Of course not. Do you really think I'd do what I did if I was?'

'I don't know, do I? I don't know you. You aren't allowing me the chance.'

'Well, I wouldn't.'

She sounded outraged and Will made himself calm down. Not everyone had infidelity forever at the forefront of their mind. 'No. Sorry.'

'Would *you*?' she snapped.

A chill rippled through him. 'No.'

'Well, then.'

'So?' What was her problem? God, he wished he could see her face.

'It's really nothing,' she said irritatingly coolly. 'Like I said, I just don't think it would work out, that's all.'

Will frowned as his stomach churned. With pique, of

course, because he couldn't remember the last time a woman had cancelled a date with him. Women generally didn't. So why was Bella giving up on them before they'd even started? And why did he even care?

Will narrowed his eyes and switched his brain into gear. This was nuts. Why was he worrying about this? So what if the fact that she'd reduced the episode in his car to a one-night stand left a bad taste in his mouth? If it didn't bother her why did it have to bother him?

Setting his jaw, he pulled himself together. He hadn't begged for a date in his life, and he wasn't about to start now.

'Fine,' he said, as if he couldn't care one way or the other. 'If that's what you want, fine.'

'Oh,' she said, sounding faintly taken aback at his capitulation. Ha. As if he was going to put up a battle. 'Well. Good. No hard feelings?'

His whole body tightened as the memory of exactly how hard she'd got him feeling smacked him around the head, and for a split second he wanted, no, *yearned*, to fight that battle. And then he ruthlessly stamped it all back down, because that kind of perverse way of thinking would lead to nothing but the sort of complications in his life that he really didn't need. Nevertheless... 'Bad choice of words, Bella.'

Another pause. 'I see,' she said. 'Yes. Sorry... Well, then, goodbye.'

'Goodbye,' he said curtly, and hung up.

Maybe it was for the best, he thought, tossing his phone on the desk in frustration. If simply cancelling their date had this effect on his equilibrium, imagine what else she could achieve.

In fact, he ought to be *glad* that she'd put an end to their acquaintance. The last thing he needed right now was a woman playing havoc with his head. Not that they ever did, of course.

It was probably the fact that he'd been too busy to go out

with a woman in the last couple of months that was messing with his mind. Yes, that was undoubtedly it, he thought, snatching his phone back up and scrolling through his list of contacts. What the hell. If he wanted a date he knew plenty of women who'd be only too pleased to hear he was back in the country and free on a Saturday night.

There was nothing special about Bella.

Absolutely nothing at all.

CHAPTER SEVEN

WILL had ruined her for ever, Bella thought morosely, taking a sip of champagne and resisting the temptation to down her glass in one. That was the only possible explanation.

Because Phoebe had been right. Alex's friend, who'd turned out not to be Will of course, but Sam, was attractive, intelligent and witty. He was interesting, good company and he'd brought her to a restaurant she'd been dying to try out ever since she'd read about it in a magazine a week or so ago. He'd kept his eyes on her face, had ordered vintage champagne and had told her the evening was on him and that she was to have whatever she wanted.

He was absolutely perfect.

Except for one thing. One tiny weeny little thing that shouldn't have bothered her in the slightest but now, apparently, did. A lot.

And that was the complete absence of any chemistry whatsoever.

Bella bit her lip as frustration clutched at her stomach. Up until a couple of days ago she'd been perfectly happy to sacrifice mind-blowing orgasms in favour of long-term commitment. Up until a couple of days ago chemistry hadn't even featured on her wish list. Now, apparently, it had gone in at number two. Now, apparently, she wanted commitment *and* great sex, which was as irritating as it was scarily unattainable.

When she'd met Sam in the bar earlier she'd automatically checked him out. She'd looked into his eyes, studied his mouth, his smile and run her gaze over his body in the hope of feeling something.

But had she? No, she hadn't. Not a spark. Not a tingle. Not a shudder. She'd dug around for even the tiniest flicker of lust, but it wasn't there.

That it now seemed to matter was infuriating in the extreme. Particularly since it was, she knew, all down to Will and the lingering effect he seemed to have on her.

With hindsight she should have simply sent him a text instead of calling. At the time though, texting, after what they'd been up to, had somehow seemed a little cowardly. Now however, she wished she hadn't been quite so principled.

The last forty-eight hours had been a nightmare. Ever since he'd abruptly hung up on her she'd barely slept. Barely been able to eat. And as for work, well, that had been a complete disaster.

Yesterday she'd been working on an emerald pendant, and without warning the fiercely intense expression on Will's face as he thrust deep inside her had flown into her head. As desire had bolted through her her vision had blurred, her hand had trembled and the emerald had shattered.

After that Bella had stuck to paperwork. Which might have been safer for her profit margin, but still didn't stop her mind wandering.

As much as she told herself that she'd done the right thing by terminating any further contact with Will, it hadn't stopped her from thinking about him constantly. It hadn't stopped her mentally adding thick dark hair, deep blue eyes and a firm muscled body, along with sizzling chemistry, to her wish list.

And it hadn't stopped her from feeling ever so slightly put out that he'd given in quite so easily.

Which was so mind-bogglingly absurd it was certifiable. Because what had she expected after she'd bailed on him? That he'd *beg* her to go out with him? Huh. She doubted Will Cameron had ever begged for anything in his life. And even if he had, she still wouldn't have gone out with him.

So why was she being so contrary? Why was he so hard to put out of her head? Why was she finding it so difficult to move on?

Sam's phone call yesterday evening should have been the perfect chance. The invitation to dinner couldn't have come at a better time and she'd fallen on it like a single female wedding guest landing on the bride's bouquet, saying yes with such effervescent enthusiasm that he'd probably got completely the wrong idea.

Agh. Bad simile, Bella thought as her head began to swim at the images that weddings and bride's bouquets and saying yes in the context of Will conjured up. Resisting the urge to hit herself over the head with the menu, she set her jaw and harnessed her self-possession. She really had to get a grip. She'd had quite enough of this pointless fixation with Will. Will was long gone. She had to focus on the future.

And the present, come to think of it. She was here with Sam now and even if their date wasn't going to go anywhere she owed it to him to make more of an effort.

Feeling slightly ashamed at quite how far she'd drifted from the conversation, Bella blinked and snapped her brain back to the man sitting opposite her telling her about…well, about something.

'I'm so sorry,' she said, aware that he was looking at her

as if expecting some kind of contribution. 'What were you saying?'

'Nothing particularly interesting,' he said, giving her a dry smile and sitting back.

Bella felt her cheeks grow warm and inwardly grimaced. She was hardly the most scintillating date Sam could have hoped for. Pulling herself together, she flashed him a bright smile. 'Oh, I'm sure that's not true,' she said.

'Believe me, it is.' He tilted his head and regarded her thoughtfully. 'I've bored you into oblivion, haven't I?'

'Of course not.' And it was true. 'It's just been a—ah—knackering week.' Which was also true. 'Sorry.'

'Look,' he said, putting down his glass after a few long, awkward seconds and leaning forwards a little. 'How about we cut straight to the chase?'

Bella felt her stomach flutter with trepidation. 'OK,' she said a little warily.

'It's not happening, is it?'

'What isn't?'

'Us.'

She let out the breath she hadn't even realised she'd been holding. 'I'm afraid not. Do you mind?'

'Not in the slightest.' He smiled. 'There's no…' He paused, as if searching for the right word.

'Zing?' Bella supplied helpfully.

'Quite.' Sam grinned. 'There's no zing, is there?'

'None at all, I'm afraid.'

Plenty of zing between her and Will though. A shiver ran down her spine and desire began to throb in the pit of her stomach. With a superhuman effort, Bella blocked it out and told herself to get a grip. If she was ever going to stand a chance of moving on she *had* to stop thinking about him.

'Good,' said Sam. 'Well, now that's cleared up, we can

enjoy supper without worrying if either of us is going to make a move.'

Bella made herself relax, grinned and picked up her menu. 'I couldn't agree more.'

The main thing he'd forgotten about Rosie Green, Will reflected as he helped his date out of her coat and handed it to the maître d', was that while she was beautiful and intelligent, like the wisteria that climbed up the back wall of Hawksley House she had a ferocious tendency to cling.

From the moment he'd picked her up, she'd been hanging on his arm and snuggling up to him, and if it hadn't been for the fact that he had no intention of sitting at the house brooding about his non-date with Bella he'd have made up some sort of excuse and got rid of her.

Quite apart from the fact that he'd been the one to ask *her* out and so ditching her would have been extremely ungentlemanly, Will decided he'd done enough brooding already. More than enough, in fact, and he was sick to the back teeth of it. So Bella hadn't wanted to go on a date with him. Big deal. He really ought to have got over it by now.

But had he? Not one little bit.

Of course, getting over it would be a hell of a lot easier if he could stop thinking about her.

It would be one thing if she confined herself to haunting him in his dreams, he thought, watching the waiter scoop up a couple of menus then indicate that they should follow him. He could just about cope with waking up hot and sweating and stiff with desire. After all, that was what cold showers were for, weren't they?

But did she do the decent thing and stick to his dreams? No, she did not. She wasn't that considerate. She popped into his head all the damn time, seizing control of his body and derailing his train of thought as she wrapped herself around him, shot him smouldering smiles and squirmed against him.

Over the past two days he'd been asked if he was all right more times than he could remember, and it was driving him insane.

'Will, are you OK?'

God. Gritting his teeth and biting back the urge to snap, Will jerked his head round to see Rosie glancing up at him, a tiny frown creasing her forehead.

'Fine,' he muttered as he always did, then plastered a smile to his face and put a hand on her back to propel her after the waiter.

Sooner or later he'd get over it, wouldn't he? Frankly, he had to, because if this tension continued he'd shatter and God only knew what would happen then. Besides the fact remained that he had asked Rosie out and she didn't deserve him to be sitting there all grim and fierce and monosyllabic.

In the vague hope that focusing on the tranquil white walls of the restaurant and the gentle music that oozed from speakers in the ceiling might soothe his poor beleaguered brain, Will let his gaze sweep around the room and with every step felt the tension ease a little.

Until his eyes landed on the couple sitting at the table next to the empty one the waiter was weaving towards.

As recognition slammed into him Will stopped dead and froze and just like that the tension rushed back. The breath shot from his lungs as if he'd been thumped in the solar plexus and the floor tilted beneath his feet.

Bloody hell.

It was Bella. With a man. Laughing and chatting and looking *extremely* cosy. All hope of tranquillity and peace vanished and his heart began to thud with something he couldn't identify.

The conversation he and Bella had had over the phone

slammed into his head. She'd told him she had plans, hadn't she? So was this why she'd cancelled their date? Because she'd had another one?

Will's eyes narrowed as they zoomed in on the man she was with. Something inside him snapped and before he could stop it a shaft of white-hot jealousy scythed through him. And then a sudden burst of anger swept through him, hot on the heels of the jealousy, and both began to churn around inside him in one seething explosive tangle.

Because hadn't she said she wasn't involved with anyone else? Hadn't she sounded outraged when he'd made the suggestion in the first place?

Well, she and whoever he was looked pretty close. Pretty damn involved.

So had she lied?

Dimly aware that he shouldn't care less if she had, Will felt his blood begin to boil. After all the lies and deceit he'd grown up with he simply couldn't help it.

'Will, is something the matter?'

Rosie's voice cut through his volatile thoughts and brought him careering back to his surroundings. 'No,' he growled, and gave her a quick smile to mitigate the tone of his voice.

She peered up at him. 'You've gone rather pale.'

'Just seen someone I wasn't expecting to,' he said tightly, forcing himself to calm down because it was fine. He was fine. And Bella, happily chatting and smiling away at her date, was certainly fine.

'Do you want to go over and say hello?'

Will frowned as his pulse picked up.

Did he?

Why not? He had no intention of leaving, and he could hardly spend the entire evening avoiding Bella and her date when they were sitting a couple of feet away. Going over and saying hello would be the mature and sensible thing to do.

Plus he'd get to see how she reacted and that would be…interesting. 'Why not?' he said coolly.

And because, despite trying to convince himself it was simply the sting of rejection, he *had* been disappointed when Bella had turned him down, and because right now he felt anything but mature and sensible, maybe not just hello.

'So how do you know Phoebe?'

Bella glanced up from the menu, rather grateful for the break. She'd spent the last few minutes trying to decide what to have and had so far narrowed it down to a choice of three. Every dish sounded too delicious for words and while Sam might have told her to order anything she liked, she doubted he'd meant *everything* she liked.

'I met her at a party about a year ago and we became friends,' she said. 'Then I started providing the gems for one of her clients who designs handbags, and now she does my PR.' Bella tapped the menu against her chin and thought that Phoebe did a lot more than just her PR. 'Actually she's more like a good friend than a colleague.' She gave him a quick smile. 'How do you know Alex?'

'We're looking at doing a joint venture together,' he said. 'Backing a start-up. Exciting if you're into that sort of thing.'

Bella grinned. 'I'll take your word for it.'

And then Sam's gaze slid over her shoulder and his eyebrows lifted and to her complete consternation the back of her neck began to prickle. Every one of her nerve endings tingled and her stomach fluttered. The sounds of the restaurant, the clinking of cutlery and the quiet hum of chatter faded. She felt a dart of alarm, a twinge of panic and then as her body began to heat the smile slipped from her face and her whole body tensed as trepidation began to wind through her.

Oh, God. Oh, no. Surely not. Not when she'd managed

to convince herself that she was moving on… That really wouldn't be fair.

But then when *was* life fair? she thought, her stomach plummeting to the floor. The back of her neck had only ever prickled once before and that had been when she'd been in the vault at the bank pretending to be completely absorbed in setting herself up and she'd sensed she wasn't alone.

As her heart began to thunder she realised that there was no use pretending she didn't know exactly who it was that Sam was staring at, who it was who was standing behind her. And it was equally no use pretending that he wasn't there.

Surreptitiously taking a deep breath and praying she'd be able to play it cool, Bella plastered a bright smile to her face and swivelled round.

To find herself staring straight at a crotch, far closer than she could have possibly imagined. And not just any old crotch, she thought, her head swimming and her heart lurching. No. This one she'd had the pleasure of before. She knew exactly what lay behind the buttons of those jeans and exactly how good it had felt inside her. As the desire that had been annoyingly elusive all evening began to pour through her she had to grip the table to stop herself slithering to the floor.

'Hello, Bella.'

Will's voice, lazy and deep, came from somewhere high above and Bella, battling back a fiery blush and ordering her heart to steady, made herself calmly lift her head.

As her eyes roamed up over the stripy shirt stretched over his chest and the chocolate brown jacket, all train of thought vanished. She couldn't even remember what was on the menu, let alone what she'd toyed with the idea of ordering. And as for playing it cool, well, that was a joke.

There was a tightness gripping his body and a hardness to the set of his mouth and her heart banged against her ribs. He looked dark and brooding, like a man on the edge. On the edge of what, she had no idea, but he was definitely teetering on the brink of something and it made her heart thump even harder.

Without warning, he bent down, brushed his lips against her cheek and Bella nearly passed out. His scent, his heat, the proximity of him stole the air from her lungs. Lust shot round her and she clamped her mouth shut to stop the whimper that was racing up her throat from escaping.

God, if she'd needed any convincing about the appeal of sexual chemistry she had it. An odd sort of buzz was spreading through her body and her blood was heating and all she knew was Will was being all grim and dark and overwhelming and she was falling under his spell all over again. Quite happily, she thought, going dizzy at the realisation.

Or rather, quite happily until she clocked the presence of the gorgeous leggy redhead draping herself over his arm.

With gritted determination Bella fought back a scowl and kept the smile in place as she ran her gaze over the woman Will was with. So much for the fleeting idea that he'd sounded annoyed when she'd cancelled their date. Unlike her, it clearly hadn't caused him any sleepless nights. He'd probably put her straight out of his mind and been on the phone to the redhead within seconds.

Huh.

She watched the redhead lean a little further into him and shoot him a smouldering smile, and she wondered whether they'd come by car and whether Will had instructed Bob to take the circuitous route.

Whether he made a habit of telling Bob to take the circuitous route.

Jealousy flooded through her and Bella had to stifle a gasp at the pain that speared her. Jealousy? What on earth was *that* all about? She had no reason to feel jealous. She was the one who'd cancelled their date, so Will could take the circuitous route with whoever he liked. Just because *she* didn't want him didn't mean that no one else would. Apart from the tiny issue with commitment he had, he was the most eligible bachelor in the country.

And besides, she'd moved on, hadn't she?

'Will,' she said, swinging her gaze back towards him and determinedly deepening her smile. 'What a surprise.'

'Isn't it?'

And then her eyes met his for the first time and she immediately wished she could dive beneath the table and stay there all night. Because his eyes were ice cold, as hard and flinty as lapiz lazuli, and cut right through her, making her shiver and putting a chill back in her blood.

He was fuming, she realised, completely poleaxed. But fuming about what? Surely he couldn't be angry with *her*, could he? All she'd done was cancel a date. Hardly the crime of the century. Yet here he was, bristling down at her, the hostility rolling off him in waves and practically drowning her. It was baffling.

'A pleasant one though,' she said, burying the lie in politeness and thinking that actually 'pleasant' was way too bland a word to associate with Will. In any context.

'Then why don't we join you?' he said with a smile so cool it was sub-zero.

What? Bella's eyebrows shot up and her stomach jumped. Oh, no. No no no no no *no*. Grabbing back some sort of control, she flashed both Will and his date an overly bright smile. 'Oh. Well, that would be delightful, of course, but I'm sure—' She glanced at the redhead.

'Rosie,' she supplied huskily.

'Rosie would rather you had your own table,' she said.

'Rosie doesn't mind,' said Will abruptly.

Rosie looked as if she minded quite a bit, but she got over it remarkably quickly and smiled graciously. 'That sounds lovely,' she said, presumably so confident that she'd have Will all to herself later that she could afford to be generous, Bella thought tartly.

'Fine by me,' said Sam, getting to his feet and summoning a waiter before Bella could shoot him a pleading look.

And then introductions were being made and a couple of waiters were hurrying over to whip off tablecloths and rearrange cutlery and crockery, and Bella felt any kind of control she might have had over events slip through her fingers like sand through an hourglass.

How was she going to get through this evening now? Enjoy supper, Sam had said. Ha. There was absolutely no chance of that. With Will in this weirdly prickly mood, and Bella feeling more than a little on edge herself, it was going to be agony.

But what could she do, apart from drum up some of that coolness and aloofness she'd hauled into action the first time she'd met Will, and count the minutes until the bill arrived?

That was it, she decided, clutching onto that idea for dear life. That was what she'd do. She'd be polite and charming, chatty when the conversation called for it, and above all she would *not* think about how the last time she'd seen Will he'd been beneath her, trapped between her thighs, clamping her against him and pounding into her.

Because he clearly wasn't, she thought darkly as he smiled down at something Rosie said with far more warmth than he'd so far offered *her* this evening.

That Will had moved on far more effectively and efficiently than she had rankled. Big time. Training her gaze on what the waiters were doing and keeping it off the couple the other side of the action, Bella made a snap decision.

Was she really going to primly sit there with Sam equally primly at her side while Will and Rosie flirted and no doubt played footsie all evening?

Was she hell.

Polite and charming be damned. If she was going to have to suffer the agonies of the next couple of hours at least she could do it on something approaching an equal basis.

'Sam?' she muttered.

'Yes?' He glanced round and bent his head towards her.

'Would you mind doing me a favour?'

If Sam touched Bella once more, thought Will grimly, he'd leap across the table, haul him up by the lapels of his very expensive-looking jacket, drag him outside and set about wiping the smile from his face. Permanently.

Ever since they'd all sat down Sam had barely been able to keep his hands off her. He'd pulled a chair out for her and planted a lingering kiss on her cheek. He'd handed her a menu, and then leaned forwards, his head touching hers as he completely needlessly pointed out the various dishes. When he'd murmured something into Bella's ear, making her laugh softly, it had taken every ounce of Will's self-control not to yank them apart and snap at them to stop acting like besotted teenagers.

'Well, isn't this a coincidence?' he said, fixing a smile to his face and looking at no one in particular.

Bella arched an eyebrow. 'Is it?' she said.

'What else would it be?'

'I read about this place in a magazine,' said Rosie. 'I've been dying to try it out.'

'So have I,' Bella muttered, sounding as if she deeply regretted it.

'And how many strings did you have to pull to get a table tonight?' said Sam, shooting Will an irritatingly conspiratorial grin.

'A few,' he said.

'Me too. But I thought, what the hell, whatever my Bella wants.'

His Bella? Bella winced a little, as well she might, and Will ground his teeth. How long had this been going on?

'So how have you been?' he said coolly, looking across the table at her.

'Absolutely marvellous,' she said, meeting his gaze equally steadily.

She looked it, he thought, running his gaze over her deliberately slowly. She looked glowing. Her hair was loose and tumbling round her shoulders and her eyes were sparkling. She was wearing a white shirt, undone just enough to provide a hint of cleavage, and caramel-coloured suede trousers that sat low on her hips and called out to be stroked.

Will curled his fingers into fists to stop them from reaching out beneath the tablecloth and doing exactly that. 'I'm so glad,' he said smoothly, thinking he was anything but.

'You?'

'Couldn't be better.'

'How nice.' She gave him a tight little smile, lifted her glass to her mouth and took a sip of champagne.

'So how do you know each other?' said Rosie, plucking a breadstick from the glass standing in the centre of the table and snapping it.

Bella jumped and spluttered and coughed, and Will felt a burst of satisfaction surge through him. She was rattled. Good. And then hot on the heels of the satisfaction came relief. Thank God he wasn't the only one to be suffering from this. For a moment there her cool detachment had been highly unnerving. But then he remembered that she'd hidden her response to him behind icy aloofness once before, and relaxed a little.

'Bella did some work for me,' he said, toying with the stem

of his own glass and watching as her eyes dipped to his fingers and darkened.

And then she'd done him.

At the thump of desire that struck him in the gut and then ricocheted around inside him Will's fingers tightened around the stem of the glass and he swiftly removed them to break the far less fragile bread roll sitting on his side plate.

'That's right,' she said calmly, although his senses, hyperalert where she seemed to be concerned, picked up on the fact that her breathing had quickened slightly and a faint flush was creeping into her face.

'She's very talented,' said Sam, throwing an admiring smile in Bella's direction that Will wanted to knock off his face.

'She certainly is,' Will murmured.

'What do you do?' asked Rosie.

Bella blinked, then smiled. 'I'm a jeweller.'

'Is the necklace you're wearing one of your designs? It's very beautiful.'

Will's gaze dipped to the amber pendant that nestled in Bella's cleavage and his mouth went dry.

Bella opened her mouth to answer and then Sam, damn him, was leaning forwards and smiling into her eyes and saying, 'I gave it to her, didn't I, darling?'

Darling? Will went so rigid he nearly shattered.

'Oh—er—yes,' said Bella, smiling right back and batting her eyelids up at him. 'Sam's so thoughtful like that.'

Will forced his jaw to relax and wished he were unscrupulous enough to use Rosie to wind Bella up as much as she was unknowingly winding him up. 'I'm sure he is.'

'I'd love something like that,' said Rosie, her voice dreamy but her eyes shooting Will a pointed look that he chose to ignore, as he always did in the face of such not-very-subtly-dropped hints.

Instead he muttered something non-committal and watched through narrowed eyes as Sam stretched his arm along the back of Bella's chair and began massaging her shoulder.

'And what about you, Rosie?' said Sam.

'I'm a professor of astrophysics at Imperial College.'

Bella's jaw nearly hit the floor and Will felt another stab of satisfaction.

'Wow,' she muttered. 'That sounds fascinating.'

Rosie shrugged and smiled modestly. 'I enjoy it. I specialise in stellar dynamics and galaxy formation. It's kind of fun.'

'And Will's a duke,' said Bella, turning to Sam.

Sam's eyebrows lifted. 'Really?'

She nodded. 'He has houses all over the country but chooses to live in the Cayman Islands. He dives.'

Curiosity spiked through him. 'You seem to know a lot about me.' Had she checked him out?

'I do.'

So what else did she know? And did any of it have anything to do with why she'd cancelled their date?

'Then you'll know I'm not only a duke,' he said.

'No.'

'What else do you do?' asked Sam.

'I trade.'

'So do I,' Sam said, eventually sliding his hand from Bella's shoulder to butter his roll. 'Who for?'

'Myself.' And because he realised he really had to relax before his blood pressure shot through the roof, Will made himself dredge some sort of small talk and said, 'How about you?'

'Parker, Collins and Black.'

Will gave a brief nod of recognition. 'Good company.'

'Why the Cayman Islands?' asked Bella.

Because of the tax benefits? Because of the diving?

Because he could leave his house unlocked without worrying about anyone breaking in? Or all of the above?

Hmm. Will might have decided to make a bit more of an effort in the way of conversation but no way was he going into all that. 'I like the heat,' he said eventually, staring straight at Bella and watching the flush in her cheeks deepen. 'Don't you?'

Something flickered in the depths of her eyes and she swallowed. And then she pulled her shoulders back, sat up a little straighter and flashed him a bright smile. 'Not a bit of it,' she said lightly. 'I hate the heat.'

'Really?' He lifted his eyebrows and shot her a smouldering smile. 'I'd have thought you'd have loved it.'

Her eyes widened. 'I can't imagine where you'd get that idea.'

'You seem that kind of woman.'

For a moment, everything else ceased to exist. For a moment it was just the two of them, enveloped in a bubble of heat and electricity and vibrating tension. Will arched an eyebrow. Curved his lips into the barest hint of a smile all the time wondering who exactly she was trying to convince.

Bella caught her lip with her teeth, then blinked and looked away. 'Well, I assure you, I'm not.'

The urge to push it, to carry on needling her until she was forced to acknowledge the chemistry between them was so strong, so insistent that it brought him slamming back to his senses. Hauling himself under control, Will shrugged and frowned and made himself back off. 'My mistake.'

'The Arctic's my kind of thing,' she said firmly. 'The colder the better.'

'I agree,' said Sam, 'which is why I'm taking her skiing in a few weeks. The Alps, I was thinking. Log fires and whisky macs. Sheepskin rugs and Bella.' He smiled. 'What more could a man want?'

Will's jaw almost snapped. Skiing? Log fires and whisky macs? Sheepskin rugs? What the hell was going on? 'What indeed?' he muttered.

'Personally I vastly prefer the heat,' said Rosie, fluttering her eyelashes at Will. 'I'd love to visit the Cayman Islands,' she added wistfully, and planted a hand on his thigh.

He tensed, was about to remove it when he saw Bella's gaze drop to it and a tiny frown pucker her forehead. Ha, he thought, and decided to leave it there.

'Perhaps Will will take you,' said Bella, lifting her eyes to his.

Not a chance. 'Perhaps,' he murmured and wondered if he might have accidentally stepped into some sort of parallel universe.

'Have you known each other long?' asked Rosie.

'A couple of weeks,' said Sam with a shrug. 'Not long, I know, but it's been pretty intense, hasn't it, honey?'

At first the implication of Sam's words didn't register. Bella's knee had bumped against his and a jolt of electricity was shooting straight to his groin, making his body tighten with need and his pulse race.

And then the words filtered through the hazy fog in his head and Will felt as if he'd been punched in the stomach. Desire vanished. Heat turned to ice.

Two weeks? His gut churned and a strange kind of numbness began to seep through him. Two weeks?

So she *had* lied.

For a few long moments a taut kind of silence descended over the table. Will stared at her, watching her expression fill with distress and her eyes cloud, and steeled himself against the unwelcome effect he suspected her reaction could have on him if he let it.

Of course she was distressed, he thought grimly. She'd been caught out.

And then, with a demonstration of self-control he migh have admired had he not been so furious, Bella pulled he shoulders back, smoothly rose to her feet and cast them al a cool smile.

'Please do excuse me,' she said, and ran for the bathroom

CHAPTER EIGHT

OH GOD, oh God, oh God.

Bella rested her burning forehead against the mirror but it did nothing to cool the heat and the turmoil churning through her body.

Gripping the edge of the vanity unit to stop herself from shaking quite so uncontrollably, she drew back and stared at her reflection. Her face was as white as the napkin she'd just thrown down, and her eyes looked huge and troubled.

Not that that was any surprise. Tonight was turning out to be the most horrendous night she'd ever had. The whole evening was hurtling out of control and she had no idea how to stop it.

And it was all entirely her own fault.

How *could* she have thought that asking Sam to pretend to be mad about her, to hang onto her every word and appear to be unable to keep his hands off her was a good idea? Since when had she played that kind of game? Shame battered its way into the tangle of emotions racing around inside her, and Bella stifled a groan.

Had she *completely* lost the plot?

It had seemed like such an excellent plan at the time, when she'd been so wrong-footed and ill at ease, but with hindsight it was childish and knee-jerkingly stupid.

Releasing her death grip on the edge of the sink, Bella

locked her knees and dug around in her handbag for her lip
gloss.

Why, oh, why couldn't Sam have told her she was out of
her tiny little mind and refused point-blank, instead of glancing over at Will and Rosie, grinning and saying sure, why
not?

And why had he had to embrace the role with quite such
enthusiasm?

Every time he'd touched her, or even smiled at her, she'd
sensed Will's tension level rocket, and had to bite back the
urge to snap at Sam to cut it out.

But then Will had started talking about heat and things,
and *her* tension level had shot up and she'd found herself
wanting to encourage Sam.

Rosie with her possessive hand planting hadn't helped.
Bella had seen the none-too-subtle movement—and Will's
lack of reaction—and it had nearly crucified her. She would
have to be a professor of bloody astrophysics, wouldn't she?
Bella thought glumly, applying a layer of gloss to her lips.
Why couldn't she have been a vacuous model or something?
Why did she have to have legs up to her armpits, a killer fig-
ure, a mane of shiny red hair *and* brains?

God, it wasn't fair.

And actually neither was she, she acknowledged, her hand
stilling as she paused and frowned at her reflection. It wasn't
really Rosie's fault there was all this tension crashing around,
and nor was it Sam's. In fact if it hadn't been for those two,
conversation, at least of the verbal kind, would have been
pretty thin on the ground.

Besides, she didn't believe in the fairness—or lack of—
of life. She believed you were in charge of your own destiny
and made your own choices. So her current predicament was
entirely of her making.

However, being aware of that didn't make it any less awful.

id it? she thought as the scene she'd fled flew into her mind
nd sent a fresh wave of nausea rolling around her stomach.
When Sam had blithely announced that they'd been seeing
ach other for two weeks she'd seen Will blanch and had
nown what he'd have thought. And then his eyes had drilled
nto hers, demanding an explanation, and, what with the heat
nd the desire and the confusion churning around inside her,
he hadn't been able to stand it any longer.

So here she was. Hiding in the loos and wishing she could
tay here for ever because she had the terrifying feeling that
ooner or later all this pressure was bound to explode, and
he wasn't sure she was prepared to face the consequences.

But what choice did she have?

The bathroom window was far too small to escape through
nd she really couldn't stay in here for ever. Her only option
vas to go out and face the music that she'd composed.

Taking a deep breath, Bella dropped her lip gloss back in
er bag and ran her wrists under the tap. Then she pulled her
houlders back and practised a smile until it looked as natural
s it ever was going to look, pinched her cheeks and shook
er hair back.

There, she told herself. That would have to do. Her insides
night be a mess, but at least she *looked* calm and in control.

All she had to do now was go out, plead a headache and
sk Sam to find her a taxi, because she didn't think she could
eep up the pretence any longer. The idea of having to con-
inue with the charade and suffering more of Will's glares
nd Rosie's sultry smiles made her smile wobble a little, and
er head started pounding so fiercely that she realised she
vouldn't even have to fake the pain.

Briefly closing her eyes and massaging her temples, Bella
traightened her spine, lifted her chin and opened the door.

To find Will leaning against the wall opposite, his hands

in his pockets, his eyes dark and impenetrable and his ex
pression grim.

Bella froze, her hand tightening on the door handle an
her heart banging against her ribs. 'Will,' she said, as cooll
as she could manage.

'Bella.'

'What are you doing here?'

A muscle in his jaw began to pound. 'You know perfectl
well.'

Bella felt a shiver scuttle down her spine. 'I'm afraid
have no idea what you mean,' she said, resisting the urge t
retreat and slam the door. Because what would that achieve
A closed door to the ladies' loos was hardly an effective de
terrent against a man like him.

Will pushed himself off the wall, stalking towards her unt
he stood in front of her like a dark immovable mountain, hi
jaw tight and his eyes glittering. 'Two weeks?'

Oh. Her chin jutted up. 'What about it?'

'How about this?' he said, pulling her to one side to let
woman go into the bathroom, planting his hands on the wal
either side of her head and wiping out her oxygen. 'Were yo
or were you not going out with Sam when we had sex on th
back seat of my car?'

In an effort to ignore the way the skin of her arms burne
from where he'd touched her, the memories ricocheting
around her head, and that gorgeous mouth, a mere inch o
two from hers, Bella channelled indignation. 'I can't believ
you want to discuss this now.'

'What else would we be likely to discuss?' he said, sound
ing as if he were gritting his teeth. 'The weather?'

Hmm. Perhaps he did have a point. And it was pretty obvi
ous he wasn't planning on letting her go until she explained

For a second Bella dithered. It was so tempting to shoo
him a killer look, say yes, duck beneath one arm and sashay

f. That would certainly put an end to everything, wouldn't
? But then what would that make her?

Yet if she said no, she'd have to explain why she and Sam
ad been all over each other all evening, and that would be
ne hell of an awkward conversation.

Will's eyes bored into hers as he waited for an answer.

Stifling a sigh, Bella gave in. For all her faults she wasn't
coward. And did she really want Will thinking she was an
nfaithful trollop who went round having quickies with any
1an who came her way? She did not. So awkward conversa-
on it would have to be.

Forcing herself to look him in the eye, Bella straightened
er spine. 'No,' she said calmly. 'I wasn't.'

Some of the tension eased from his body and he drew back
little. 'Are you going out with him now?'

'No,' said Bella, feeling as if she could breathe again. 'We
nly met this evening.'

'So why have you spent the last twenty minutes letting me
1ink you were?'

She shrugged and studied the huge abstract painting on
ne wall behind him. 'It seemed like a good idea at the time.'

He frowned. 'Why?'

'I'm not sure.'

'Well, work it out,' he snapped.

Bella jumped and her hackles shot up. Did he *really* imag-
1e that she was going to divulge the jealousy, the frustra-
on, the longing that had made her ask Sam to pretend to be
1volved with her? Or the constant pummelling disappoint-
1ent that with his issues with commitment Will would never
e the right man for her? *No* chance.

'Anyone would think you're jealous,' she said, deciding that
ttack was the best way to deal with that particular problem,
nd giving him a mocking little smile.

For a second there was silence. Then Will sprang back

and raked his hands through his hair, his eyes blazing. 'C
course I'm bloody jealous,' he said, so fiercely that Bel
gasped. 'Two days ago you were writhing on top of me an
now you're out for dinner the evening we were supposed t
be going out wrapped around another man.'

'You're not exactly sitting at home pining,' she shot bac
unable to keep an odd trace of hurt out of her voice at th
thought of the beautiful Rosie and where she'd had her hand

'Now who's the one sounding jealous?'

'I'm not jealous,' she snapped. 'Just pointing out the facts

Will let out a sharp hollow laugh. 'Oh, give up the game
Bella.'

Bella bristled and battled back a wince of shame becaus
shame had no place in this conversation. 'What games? I
anyone's playing games, it's you, Will. You started this whe
you decided to come over and say hello and then embarke
on a two-tiered conversation.'

'No. *You* started this when you cancelled our date for n
apparent reason.'

'I had my reasons,' she said, glaring at him.

'Which are?'

Bella set her jaw. 'Never mind.'

Will swore beneath his breath. 'Don't you think you ow
me an explanation?'

She folded her arms over her chest and stuck her chin u
'No.'

Will took a step back and clenched his fists as if to sto
himself from shaking her and for a moment they bristled a
each other in silence.

The door opened and Bella jumped. The woman who'
gone in earlier came out, glanced at each of them in turr
avid curiosity spread all over her face, and then darted off a
if worried she might catch some of the fraught tension swirl
ing around the place.

The interruption lasted only a matter of seconds, but it was ᵊough to break the stand-off.

'You know,' said Will with a sigh as he frowned and rubbed ᵊhand along his jaw, 'I never play games.'

Bella's mouth went dry and she swallowed. 'Neither do I,' ᵊe said, her voice sounding annoyingly husky. 'I've always ᵊought them a complete waste of time.'

'Me too.' He glanced at her. 'Yet here we are, playing ᵊames with each other like it's a matter of life and death. ᵊhy do you think that is?'

Her breath caught in her throat. 'I don't know.'

He took a step towards her. 'Yes, you do.'

She did. And wasn't that exactly the trouble?

Feeling all the energy drain out of her, Bella sighed and ᵊn her hands through her hair. 'Look, Will,' she said wearily, ᵊ'm sorry for making you think that there was more to Sam ᵊnd me than there is. I'm sorry your evening's been ruined. ᵊut I have a headache and I want to go home.'

Will paused and frowned. 'OK. Then I'll take you. We can ᵊlk on the way there.'

Oh, no. Not a chance. 'No.' She put up a hand and gave ᵊim a quick smile. 'Thank you. But I'll be fine. We don't ᵊave anything left to talk about and, besides, you have a date ᵊho, I'm sure, is looking forward to being taken the circu-ᵊous route home.'

Will tensed. 'What the hell does that mean?' he said in a ᵊangerously low voice.

God. Why couldn't she have kept her mouth shut and just ᵊft? Bella's heart began to thump. His eyes burned into her, ᵊemanding an explanation all over again and she realised that ᵊny closure that they might have been working towards had ᵊvaporated.

With her mouth firing off without her consent, she needed ᵊ leave before she said or did something she really might regret. 'Oh, nothing,' she said making a move to march off and then having to halt when Will blocked her.

'Right,' he said sardonically.

Bella's hackles shot up. 'Do you mind…?'

'Yes, I do.'

Her stomach knotted with nerves and alarm and a million other things she wasn't sure she wanted to acknowledge. 'So what are you planning to do?' she said, looking up at him and fixing a cool little smile to cover up all the unsettling emotions spinning around inside her. 'Use your superior physical strength to get what you want?'

Will went still and a muscle started ticcing in his jaw and Bella's skin prickled with panic. God. What was she doing baiting him like this? Was she nuts?

'I wouldn't have to,' he said, taking a step towards her and slowly and deliberately lowering his gaze to her mouth.

Her throat as dry as if she'd swallowed every grain of sand in the Sahara, Bella swallowed hard and raced through her options. Telling him what she'd meant would be mortifying, yes, but a damn sight safer than being on the receiving end of one of Will's spine-tingling kisses, which was undoubtedly what he was talking about.

'OK,' she said with an indifferent shrug. 'Fine. All I meant was that, for all I know, you might make a habit of ravishing women on the back seat of your car.'

For a second there was silence. Will visibly reeled and as he went pale Bella experienced a brief pang of remorse.

Which vaporised the instant his reaction elbowed its way to the surface.

'What the hell?' he roared, his eyes glittering and his hand clenching. 'God, you push too far, Bella.'

Bella lifted her chin and, with as little control over her behaviour as a train careering off the rails, pushed again. 'I can't help but notice you haven't addressed my point.'

'I can't believe you have to ask.'

'I can't believe you haven't answered.'

Will hauled himself under control as if remembering where they were. 'Of course I don't make a habit of ravishing women in the back seat of my car,' he ground out. 'You were the first. And, frankly, I hope, the last. Because every bloody time I go anywhere in it, it all comes rushing back to me and I have to get Bob to pull over and let me out. Which would be fine if I was in any state to walk.' His eyes blazed. 'But the memory of you, of what we did, makes walking pretty bloody impossible. You think I'd want to repeat that?'

'Oh.' Bella blinked, too shell-shocked by what he'd just said to know how to respond. 'Well. Good.'

'Good? *Good?* It isn't good. It's hell on earth. I can't stop thinking about you. You're in here,' he growled, jabbing at his temple, 'all the damn time. And you've been so bloody glacial and aloof and distant this evening, it's been driving me nuts.'

'Oh,' she said again. 'Sorry.'

'Are you?' he grated. 'Really?' He closed the distance between them and her heart began to thunder. 'Then make it up to me,' he muttered, planting one hand on the wall beside her head, pinning her to the wall with his hips and slamming his mouth down on hers.

Bella didn't have a chance to protest even if she'd wanted to. Which she didn't. Because actually she wasn't sorry in the slightest. She was stunned. Thrilled. And desperately relieved.

Her lips parted automatically beneath the hot hard pressure of his mouth and his tongue thrust between them. As her arms wound around his neck her mind went blank and she turned into one mass of quivering sensation.

Teeth clashing, his tongue tangled with hers, stroking and caressing her while his hand slid from the wall to her head and buried itself in her hair. Her heart hammered, desire flooded through her and she moaned.

'I knew it,' he muttered, breaking off the kiss to slide his mouth along her jaw and then down the side of her neck. 'So much heat. So much better than all that horrible iciness.'

Bella dropped her head back and arched against him, revelling in the feel of all that muscle, all that hardness and strength plastered against her.

His mouth found hers again and his hand slid up her side to curve round and cup her breast. Bella groaned, pressed herself closer and rubbed herself against him, so desperate with the need to feel him deep inside her that she didn't give a damn about where they were.

'God, how could you even think about cancelling our date when there's this?' he muttered against her mouth.

And just like that, Bella froze, his words obliterating the desire consuming her as effectively as any bucket of cold water.

Oh, God. What was she doing? Clinging to him like a limpet, wrapping herself around him like an octopus and kissing him as if he were the last man alive.

More to the point, what was she *thinking*? What had happened to the assurances she'd made to herself that she was no longer interested in Mr Right Now? And wasn't she supposed to have moved on? Ha. If she hadn't just had such a big wake-up call, the furthest she'd have moved on would have been to the nearest private horizontal surface.

Desire flooded back at the thought of getting naked and horizontal with Will, and Bella swallowed as her body began to tremble. Lord, it would be so easy to give in. To sink against him and say yes to the demands his body, and hers, were making. So easy to let him take her home and make love to her all night. And so easy to embark on a torrid no-strings affair.

But that wasn't what she wanted, was it?

'Bella?'

Summoning up a strength she hadn't known she possessed, she put a hand on his chest. 'Stop,' she said, her voice sounding breathy and husky as if she'd just tumbled out of bed. 'We have to stop.'

Will lifted his head and took a step back, his eyes dark and glazed. 'You're right,' he said, dragging his hands through his hair and nodding briefly. 'This isn't the time, and it really isn't the place.'

'No,' she said, more firmly this time. 'I mean we can't do this.'

He stilled. Looked at her in disbelief. 'Are you serious?'

'Deadly.'

'I see.' His brows snapped together. 'And why exactly can't we do this?'

'It's complicated.'

'What's complicated about it?' he said, all traces of passion evaporating. 'I want you and you want me. What could be simpler?'

'I wish it *was* simple,' she said, her heart sighing with longing while her body yelled that it was precisely that simple.

Will thrust his hands into his pockets and let out a deep sigh of frustration. 'I don't understand.'

Of course he didn't, she thought with some despair. Why would he be aware of the turmoil churning around inside her? Or the battle that raged between her body and her head? The battle that if she wasn't really careful her head could well end up losing. She barely understood it herself.

But there was one thing she did understand. And that was that Will had been right. She *did* owe him an explanation. More than that, after the stupid games she'd tried to pretend she hadn't been playing, she owed him the truth.

* * *

Will watched Bella pull her shoulders back and set her jaw and felt like giving himself a good kicking. Why, oh, why had he had to say anything? If he'd kept his mouth glued to hers instead of foolishly using it to express what he was thinking, he was pretty sure that he and Bella would now be ensconced in the cupboard he'd spotted earlier, and satisfying the craving that he knew clawed away at both of them.

Instead he had a stomach-sinking feeling that the only thing going to be satisfied this evening was his curiosity.

Dredging up enough control to rein in the desire still rocketing around inside him Will frowned and braced himself for whatever was coming.

'Tell me, Will,' she said, her face so earnest that he was tempted to haul her back into his arms and set about switching it back to flushed and dazed, 'where do you see this going?'

He tensed. Oh, yes. There went his stomach, plunging south like an anchor through water. With an ease born out of habit, he arranged his features into a mask of neutrality that didn't show even a hint of the alarm that scurried through him. 'See what going?' he said evenly.

'This.' She waved a hand between them. 'Us.'

Will frowned. 'We've only just met.'

'So?'

'So there isn't an us.' They'd never be an 'us'. He didn't do 'us'es.

She shrugged. 'Humour me.'

Will stifled a sigh. 'I don't see the point. Whatever there might have been barely started. You've seen to that.'

She tilted her head. Considered his reply. Then bit her lip and nodded. 'I see. Well, I guess that's my answer. As I suspected.'

As she suspected? What was this? Another one of her games? 'Why does it have to be going anywhere anyway?'

he said, frustration and bewilderment churning around inside him. 'What's wrong with just having incredible sex?'

'I'm not interested in incredible sex.'

'You were on Thursday.'

Her jaw tightened and she closed her eyes for a brief second. 'That was then.'

'So what's changed?'

'We want different things.'

'How on earth do you have any idea about what I want?' he said, struggling to keep a grip on his temper.

'When I got home on Thursday night, I looked you up online. That's how I know where you live and what you do. It's also how I know what you want.'

Will felt like hitting something hard. Like the wall. Because, God, this conversation was infuriating. He shoved his hands in his pockets. 'What I want with regards to what?'

'Sex and relationships. You're keen on the former. Not so much on the latter.'

Oh. Well. That much was true. His aversion to commitment was as well documented as the variety of women that had appeared on his arm over the years. It appeared he'd been right when he'd suspected she'd found out something about him she didn't like. 'And what do *you* want?' As if he couldn't guess.

'Both.' The tilt of her chin became more defiant. 'Actually, everything.'

He frowned. 'Everything?'

'I'm not interested in an affair,' she said simply. 'I've been there, done that. I'm nearly thirty-five and I now want more. I want a relationship. Commitment. Security. Ultimately marriage and a family. So I can't really afford to waste time on something, or someone, that won't at least give me the chance of having that.'

Oh, crap. Will's stomach sank even further. So his initial

impression of her hadn't been wrong after all. He might have managed to convince himself that she was the sort of woman who threw inhibition to the wind and herself at random men, but he'd been deluding himself. If he hadn't been so annoyed he'd have been relieved that his judgement hadn't gone off the rails as he'd feared.

'What's so great about commitment?' he said.

'It's what I want, what I've always wanted.'

'Why?'

'It'll give me the security I never had. The family and the roots I never had.' She took a deep breath. 'Look, my mother had something of a racy past. She was kind of wild. Mixed with the wrong crowd. When I was twelve she went to jail.'

He stared at her chin sticking up, daring him to be discouraged. But did she really think having a mother who went to jail would deter him? She should hear about some of *his* ancestors. 'What for?'

'Armed robbery. She was involved in a jewellery heist that went wrong. She spent seven years inside.'

'Sounds intriguing.'

Bella frowned. 'Yes, well, it wasn't to me. It was awful. I ended up being shunted from one place to the next, never really being in one place long enough to settle.'

'What about your father?'

She bit her lip. 'I have no idea who my father is. Neither does my mother.'

'Fathers can be overrated,' Will muttered, his thoughts momentarily derailed by the images of a young Bella trudging forlornly from one place to the next that were now flying around his head and making his chest contract in the strangest way.

'I agree. But I could have done with one, especially during my teens. On the whole I was well looked after.' She shrugged. 'I guess I ended up hating always being on the move and constantly living out of a suitcase. I certainly hated the lack of stability.'

'Commitment doesn't necessarily mean stability,' Will said as the knowledge he held about his ancestors flashed across his mind. 'Or security.'

'It does to me. So you see that's why I had to cancel our date. This… You and me… Whatever it is…would never work.' Bella shrugged and caught her lower lip with her teeth.

Completely transfixed by her mouth, Will reached forwards, cupped her jaw and ran his thumb over her lip. She let out an involuntary gasp and desire roared through his body. 'You think?' he murmured.

'I know,' she said sharply, jerking back.

Will dropped his hand before he could slide it to the back of her neck, pull her against him again and make a mockery of her assertion and simply stared at her, his pulse hammering.

Who was she trying to kid? It wouldn't work? That was the most nonsensical thing he'd ever heard. Of course it would work. They were dynamite together. Totally explosive. Did she even know how rare the kind of chemistry that they shared was? Not to indulge in it, however briefly, would be a crime against nature.

All he had to do was get her to see things his way. Show her that a short-term fling needn't interfere with her long-term goals. Or his.

Will's mind raced as desire and need drowned out reason and logic. Oh, he had no doubt it wouldn't be easy. Bella wasn't going to change her mind, roll over and hand herself to him on a plate. But that merely added to the challenge, and he'd never been one to shy away from a challenge.

Attrition. That was the thing. He'd gradually erode her resistance until she was desperate, begging him to make love to her and willing to agree to anything he suggested.

'I see your point,' he said as adrenalin surged through him at the thought of having Bella in his arms, panting and pleading for release.

'There are bound to be hundreds of other women out there you can have incredible sex with.'

'Bound to be,' he said vaguely, his brain switching into gear and formulating a plan. Because if this evening had clarified anything it was that right now he didn't want sex, incredible or otherwise, with anyone else. He wanted it with her. Lots of it.

'Oh,' she said, blinking and sounding delightfully taken aback. 'Good. Well. I'm glad you agree.'

'I couldn't agree more.' He flashed her a grin and wrapped his hand round her elbow. 'Now I think we should be getting back before someone sends out a search party, don't you?'

CHAPTER NINE

THE following morning, after twelve hours of solid sleep, Bella felt like a different person. All was now well with the world. At least with *her* world, which she'd chosen to decorate with denial and to view through rose-tinted spectacles.

After the turbulent conversation and mind-blowing kiss outside the loos, she and Will had gone back into the restaurant to find the table empty. The waiter removing the empty glasses and the unused cutlery had murmured discreetly that their dining companions had given up waiting and had informed him that Will and Bella would take care of the bill.

Will, as surprisingly unperturbed by this as he'd been by her revelations about her parentage, had brushed aside all her efforts to at least split the bill, and had handed over his card. Then he'd bundled her into a taxi as if he couldn't get rid of her fast enough, and had vanished into the night.

Very possibly to go straight round to Rosie's to get some of that incredible sex she'd stupidly assured him others would be only too happy to provide.

God, what on earth had possessed her to say *that*? she wondered, switching the oven on and taking a couple of croissants from the freezer. She'd only tossed it into the conversation as a throwaway comment, so naturally it was the one thought that had dominated her journey home.

As much as she'd tried to tell herself that she really couldn't care less, she'd arrived home slightly confused, greatly un-settled, and too exhausted to do anything other than flop into bed and pass out.

But this morning she was revived. Ravenous, but revived. And heartily relieved that everything was back to normal. Because it was, wasn't it?

And if a tiny part of her was still a bit preoccupied by the idea of Will and Rosie together, and if another even tinier part of her was faintly put out that Will had agreed with her about the futility of pursuing any kind of relationship with her with quite such alacrity, well, it was simply hunger messing with her head. That was all.

Bella dropped the croissants onto a tray and shoved it in the oven, her mouth watering and her stomach rumbling.

Oh, yes. All was indeed well with the world.

Except for one thing.

Bella frowned, straightened and bit her lip. As much as she was enjoying patting herself on the back at how well she'd managed to extricate herself from a situation trickier than a magicians' convention, she couldn't help but feel appalled at the shoddy way she'd treated Sam.

It had been jabbing away at her conscience all morning and as a fresh deluge of guilt washed over her her stomach churned with shame. She didn't deserve freshly brewed coffee and delicious hot buttery croissants; she deserved lukewarm water and thin grey gruel. Because basically she'd used him, hadn't she? And that had been a lousy thing to do.

Hmm. If she was to enjoy her badly needed breakfast at all, she had to fix things. Before the timer pinged.

Picking up the phone and dialling Sam's number before she had the chance to chicken out, Bella leaned against the counter and concentrated on the rings instead of the ball of nerves and shame tangling in the pit of her stomach.

'Hello?'

'Sam?' she said. 'It's Bella.'

'Ah,' he said knowingly, and she inwardly cringed. 'And how are *you* this morning?'

He sounded intrigued and Bella closed her eyes for a second. 'Fine. Better than I should be. Look, Sam, I'm so sorry about last night.'

'Don't be.'

'Please let me apologise. It was unfair of me to use you like that and I shouldn't have done it.'

'Did you see me complaining? It was the most fun I've had in years.'

Huh? Her eyes snapped open at the chuckle that came down the line. Crikey. If that was the case then he needed to get out more.

'Nevertheless,' she said, guilt still swilling around her insides, 'it was unforgivable to abandon you like that.'

'I imagine you and Will had things…to discuss.'

'We did,' Bella muttered, and determinedly ignored the memory of the exact nature of their 'discussion'. 'But that's no excuse.'

'Well, please don't worry about it. I have a date with the lovely Rosie next week so all in all I had a great night. Really.'

Oh. Relief flooded through her, although whether at the fact that Sam really didn't seem to mind or at the fact that if he and Rosie were going on a date then the odds of her and Will having spent the night together had just dropped dramatically she didn't want to know.

Whichever it was, Bella felt the anxiety gripping her body ease and blew out a breath. 'OK, if you're sure…'

'I am,' he said. 'But I appreciate the thought, so thank you. So what about you? How was your night?'

'I've had better,' Bella said dryly, and then jumped at the sound of the buzzer ricocheting through her flat. 'Hang on,' she said, clutching the phone to her chest and picking up the intercom. 'Yes?'

'It's Will.'

For a moment Bella's heart stopped and she went cold. Then it started up again at double its usual rate and she went so hot she nearly passed out.

Oh, God, she thought, her brain racing. What was *he* doing here? He was supposed to have exited her life so why had he pitched up outside her flat? Fate really did seem to have it in for her.

'What do you want?' she said, sounding none too friendly but too wired to do anything about it.

'Can I come up?'

Agh. Resisting the temptation to say no and then hide, Bella muttered beneath her breath and buzzed him in. Her heart beating annoyingly fast, she stuck the phone back to her ear. 'Sorry about that,' she said.

'I don't know whether to be shocked or impressed by your vocabulary,' said Sam. 'I take it your visitor isn't welcome.'

'Not particularly.' She sighed and briefly closed her eyes. 'I swear Will Cameron's sole purpose on this planet is to torment me.' She could hear the sound of muffled laughter coming down the line. 'It's not funny,' she said huffily.

'I think it's hilarious,' he said and she could practically see his grin.

Huh. He really did need to get out more. 'I'm delighted you think so.'

'Good luck.'

'Thanks,' she muttered. 'You too.'

Bella hung up, and, at the sound of footsteps thumping up the stairs, stalked along the hall. Resisting the urge to see what she looked like in the mirror that hung above the console table, she opened the door. It was a Sunday morning and she was off work, so Will could take her as he found her.

Ah. Maybe that wasn't such a good choice of words. A vision of Will pushing her up against the wall, ripping off her clothes and taking her exactly as he found her slammed into her head and she went dizzy.

Hmm, she thought, taking a deep breath and willing her heart rate to steady. As her brain was behaving like a loose cannon maybe she ought to disengage it. Maybe she ought to keep everything nice and easy and simply deal with the facts.

Yes, that was it. Tugging her shoulders back and setting her jaw, Bella channelled her inner calm. She'd focus on the reason he'd come and not the hope that he was planning to continue where they left off last night.

She froze, her heart skipping a beat. The hope? No, that was wrong. The fear. That was what she'd meant. Yes, the *fear* that he'd try and carry on where they'd left off. Better remember that.

'Good morning, Bella,' said Will, reaching the top of the stairs and giving her a dazzling smile.

Hmm. It would be a damn sight easier to remember that she didn't want him to continue where they left off last night if he didn't look quite so good. This morning he was wearing a battered brown leather jacket, jeans and a red jumper that looked so soft she wanted to rub her cheek against it.

And what did he have to be so cheerful about anyway? she wondered, biting on that cheek and stamping out any ideas it might have about snuggling up to his chest. Had he just come from a sexathon with Rosie? Not that she was interested, of course, and not that she'd ever ask, but still. Something had certainly put a spring in his step, and the odds they'd spent the night together—which had dropped so dramatically while she'd been on the phone to Sam—rocketed.

Utterly thrown by the weird tangle of stuff churning

around inside her on top of the dazzling smile, Bella fought
back a scowl and mustered up a bright smile of her own.

The facts, she reminded herself. Stick to the facts.

'Please, do come in,' she said, standing aside, releasing
her grip on the edge of the front door and hoping her knees
had enough strength to keep her upright.

Will brushed past her and Bella's breath caught in her
throat. God, if she'd thought he robbed her shop of oxygen,
here it felt as if the walls were imploding in the vacuum.

'Would you like some coffee?' she managed, pointing him
in the direction of her kitchen. The kitchen had windows. The
kitchen had air.

'That would be lovely.'

Will sat down and Bella busied herself pouring him a cup,
grinding her teeth and trying to ignore the sensation that his
eyes were boring into her back. 'Croissant?' she muttered,
setting the cup on the table and glancing at him.

Will shot her another smile. 'Why not?'

If he hadn't wiped all rational thought from her head, she
was pretty sure she'd have been able to think of a whole number of reasons why not. Instead, she found herself fishing the
butter from the fridge and decanting some jam into a bowl.

With breakfast set out on the table Bella sat down and ignored the fact that she couldn't remember the last time she'd
shared breakfast with a man.

'So how's Rosie this morning?' she said and went still. Oh,
damn. More interested than she'd tried to kid herself, then.
What had happened to focusing on why Will was here?

He arched an eyebrow. 'Fine.'

Bella blinked and felt as if someone had thumped her in
the stomach. So he *had* gone round to see her after he'd left
her in the restaurant. It really shouldn't hurt so much. 'I'm
so glad,' she said, her voice cracking a little. Then she ral-
lied and resisted the urge to snatch the cup of coffee from in

ront of him. 'So's Sam,' she said with a bright smile. 'Fine,
hat is.'

His jaw tightened and his eyes narrowed. 'I see.'

Several long slow seconds ticked by. 'So that's good, then.
That they're both fine, I mean.'

'Isn't it?' Will threw the contents of his cup down his
hroat, seemingly impervious to the heat.

The buzzer pinged and Bella shot to her feet as if her
chair had unexpectedly caught fire. Grabbing a tea towel, she
whipped the croissants out of the oven and slid them onto a
plate.

'So,' said Will, watching her every move, 'are you seeing
him again?'

Unlikely, seeing as he was going on a date with Rosie, but
maybe Will didn't know that. She sat back down and vaguely
waved a hand. 'Oh… Ah… Well, I might. I don't know.'

'Right.' He nodded, looked as if he was about to say something else but then changed his mind, and instead broke open
the croissant.

'What about you and Rosie?' she asked, every one of her
facial muscles aching with the effort of maintaining her smile.

'What about us?'

'Are you seeing her again? *Did* you see her again? Maybe
after you put me in the taxi?'

Will glanced up and stared at her, stunned incredulity
written all over his face. 'What? Of course I didn't.'

'Yet you know she's fine…' Dammit, why couldn't she let
this go?

'Because that's what she said when I called her this morning to apologise for leaving her in the restaurant like that.'

Bella's eyes jerked to his and relief spun through her. 'Oh,
thank heavens for that. I thought… Well, you probably don't
want to know what I thought.'

For a moment there was utter silence, then Will thumped

his hand on the table and she and the crockery jumped. 'God Bella, what kind of man do you think I am?'

Not the sort of man she'd been thinking he was, clearly. She felt herself go red and a fresh wave of mortification washed over her.

'OK, I'm sorry. I just assumed…' She trailed off and shrugged. 'Never mind.' God, what was *wrong* with her?

'I went straight home. I assumed you did too.' His jaw tightened and his face darkened ominously. 'Now, though, I find myself revising my assumption.'

'Don't,' she said quickly. 'I mean you're right. I came straight home too. And I only know that Sam's fine because I was on the phone to him earlier, when you buzzed. Apologising as well, funnily enough.'

Bella thought she heard him mutter something like 'bloody games' but then he pulled himself together and visibly relaxed. 'Did you hear they're going on a date together?'

'So I understand.'

One corner of his mouth hitched and Bella's stomach flipped. 'A couple of regular little cupids, aren't we?'

'Aren't we just.' She wrapped her hands around her cup of coffee, took a sip and reminded herself that Cupid had no business popping up anywhere where she and Will were concerned.

The facts, on the other hand… Bella set her cup back down and forced herself to concentrate. 'So why are you here, Will?'

'I need your help.'

Her eyebrows shot up. 'Oh? With what?'

'Remember my jewellery collection?'

'How could I forget it?' she said dryly.

'Quite. Well, I need to get the fake stones replaced with real ones.'

'Why?'

'Because the collection is to go on display.'

For a moment there was utter silence. Bella opened her mouth then shut it and stared at him as he calmly buttered his croissant. 'But it can't,' she said, appalled.

'I know.' He shrugged and added a dollop of jam. 'However, it is. In approximately three weeks.'

Three weeks? 'How?' she said, her head swimming with questions and bafflement. 'Why?'

Will took a bite, swallowed and sighed in appreciation. 'If you remember the collection,' he said, 'then I imagine you'll remember my aunt.'

Bella tried to focus. How could he eat at a time like this? Her own appetite, which had previously been enormous, had vanished. 'Of course.'

Will sat back and looked at her. 'I discovered last night that she promised the director of the Grayson Museum that they could exhibit the collection.'

Bella frowned. The Grayson was one of the finest private museums in the country. Under any other circumstances it would be a major coup. For both parties. Under these circumstances, however, it was a disaster of epic proportions. 'Why on earth would she do something like that?'

He raised an eyebrow. 'She has bouts of questionable judgement.'

Don't we all, thought Bella darkly as she briefly reviewed her behaviour ever since she'd met Will. 'She certainly does.'

'And apparently he was *extremely* persuasive.'

Will's tone left Bella in no doubt about the nature the man's persuasion had taken, and she fought back a blush at the memory of how persuasive *he* could be. 'Can't you say she made a mistake?'

'Unfortunately not. The deal is already done, and to withdraw now would invite questions I really wouldn't feel comfortable answering.'

'Yet you'd feel comfortable with dozens of experts lining up to take a look?'

'Not particularly.'

'Good. Because you do realise they'd know, don't you? In a second.'

Will nodded. 'That thought did occur to me, which is why I'm here. With you repairing the dodgy pieces, I figured we might just get away with it.'

Bella frowned and told herself to focus on the facts and not the bubble of delight spinning through her at his appreciation of her expertise. 'Maybe you could just not show the fakes. I don't know… Say they're lost. Or stolen or something.' Because personally she wasn't sure she shared his confidence in her abilities.

Will shook his head. 'Impossible. Caroline already told the director the collection's complete, and to have a last-minute robbery would simply invite more of those questions I'm not too comfortable answering. Not to mention a whole host of other problems.'

Bella bit her lip. 'But replacing the stones will cost a fortune.'

Will lifted a shoulder. 'The cost doesn't matter. Discretion, however, does. Which is another reason why I've come to you. The fewer people that know about this, the better.' He tilted his head and gave her a penetrating look that she felt right down to her bones. 'So. Can you do it?'

Bella blinked as her brain churned with so many questions that she couldn't pull out a single one to formulate. It was all too bizarre. Too much of a coincidence. On the one hand would Caroline *really* have promised the collection to a museum knowing the risk she'd be running? On the other, if she'd really thought she could get away with switching the gems in the first place, then her judgement was definitely questionable.

Whatever had brought it about, and frankly Bella's brain was beginning to hurt at trying to work it out, one thing was certain. The collection couldn't go on display as it was.

Slowly she nodded. 'I can.' With a little help. And then she frowned. 'When exactly does it all have to be ready?'

'The opening night is two weeks on Friday, so ideally that morning at the latest.'

Bella gulped as her stomach twisted with nerves. It would be tight, but if she sidelined her principles and all her other projects she should be able to do it. In fact, the increase in workload would no doubt make her forget the fact that the Friday he was talking about was her birthday, which would be a bonus. 'OK.'

'Good,' he said with a quick smile as he got to his feet and put the plates and cups in the sink. 'Then I'll bring the pieces over tomorrow.'

Oh. Bella stared up at him as he plucked his jacket off the back of his chair. That didn't sound so good. It was one thing trying to move on with her life and her goals when Will was nowhere to be seen, quite another if he intended to carry on popping up unexpectedly.

Never mind, she thought, trying not to notice the sliver of taut tanned abdomen between the bottom of his jumper and the waistband of his jeans that the shrugging on of his jacket revealed. Once he'd brought over the jewellery and she'd started to work on it, there'd be no reason for him to pop up anywhere, unexpectedly or otherwise. She could keep him updated on her progress by email and courier the pieces directly to the museum.

'Fine,' she murmured, standing up, heading for the front door and opening it, taking care to plaster herself against the wall so that no part of him could touch her.

Will stepped out onto the landing and fished his car keys out of his pocket.

'No Bob?' she said, letting out a breath before glancing down and then back up at him.

'Sadly not. Sunday is his day off. Sundays I have to fend for myself.'

At the look of distress in his eyes, Bella couldn't help laughing. 'Poor baby.'

Will went still and Bella's laughter died in her throat as the distress vanished and something hotter, darker, flickered in their navy depths. Her mouth went unaccountably dry and her pulse began to hammer.

'I know,' he said softly. 'I don't know how I cope.'

For a long second everything seemed to stop. All Bella was aware of was a kind of throbbing electric tension vibrating between the two of them. His gaze dipped to her mouth and she thought he leaned forwards a little.

Her heart thumped and her blood heated. Oh, God. Was he going to kiss her? What would she do if he did? Slap him across the face? Or wrap her arms around him and kiss him back? Or maybe both… Because as much as she'd tried to convince herself otherwise, and as nuts as it would be, she did want another taste of him, another long slow taste of that passion that he'd shown her last night.

And then just when she was wondering what would happen if she gave into the madness and threw herself into his arms, Will was drawing back and giving her a little smile, and Bella felt as if she were the one who'd been slapped in the face.

'I'll see you tomorrow,' he said gruffly, turning on his heel and disappearing down the stairs.

CHAPTER TEN

By THE time the opening night rolled around Bella was a jumble of nerves and exhaustion and a whole lot more besides.

The last three weeks had been testing to say the least. Not only had she been working flat out to get the pieces ready for tonight, but the memory of the kiss that Will hadn't given her outside her front door had been haunting her dreams.

In her dreams, however, he didn't stalk off and leave her quivering on the landing, desperate and frustrated. In her dreams he whisked her back inside her flat and carried her into her bedroom. In her dreams he peeled her clothes off and tied her to her wrought-iron bed-head and then used his mouth and hands and body to torment her until she was shaking and quivering and delirious with pleasure.

Sometimes the journey from her door to her bed varied: sometimes they went straight there, sometimes they detoured via the shower. Sometimes she changed the colour of the silk scarves and who was doing the tying up. But the outcome was always the same, and night after night she woke up hot and bothered and trembling with desire.

And as if the nights weren't bad enough, Will had invaded her thoughts during daylight hours as well. She'd lost track of conversations, mislaid bits of jewellery and frequently drifted off, gazing into the distance, until something snapped her back to her senses and she'd discovered that half the morning had gone.

It didn't help that he'd taken to dropping in on her every other day or so to find out how she was getting on. When she'd protested that he really didn't need to bother, he'd pointed out that the integrity of the collection was at stake and he was spending a small fortune on the replacement stones, so why wouldn't he want to bother? She hadn't had an adequate comeback to that, so she'd had to bear his visits as coolly and stoically as she could manage.

At first she'd succeeded in keeping things strictly business. She'd shown him the progress she was making, and they'd discussed the collection and how it could be displayed to show off the genuine pieces to their best advantage and minimise the risk of anyone spotting the repairs.

But over the course of the last two weeks, somehow they'd ended up talking less about the work and more about other things. Personal things.

She'd found herself telling him about her peripatetic childhood and the colourful characters that had peppered her upbringing. About how, instead of doing her homework, she'd learned to pick locks, forge cheques and hot-wire cars. Far from being appalled, as she'd rather feared, Will had been fascinated and so, encouraged, she'd gone on to tell him all about her mother and her wildly misspent youth and about how she now lived quietly in Truro, kept goats and grew herbs.

She told him how thanks to a family friend she'd got into the jewellery business and how much, after growing up surrounded by people who lied for a living, she valued honesty.

In return Will had told her about what Caroline had been getting up to online and what he got up to on the Cayman Islands. He'd regaled her with stories about some of the things *is* dodgy ancestors had got up to and had told her about the ukedom he'd inherited.

Gradually the cool, stoical air she'd adopted to deal with is visits had disappeared and she'd found herself looking forward to them instead. Clock-watching as she'd waited for him drop by. Aching with disappointment the days he didn't, which had become increasingly frequent recently. The disproportionate intensity of her reaction when he didn't come as as disconcerting as the fact she'd taken to clock-watching n the first place.

Which was almost as unsettling as the dawning realisaon that she didn't only fancy him rotten; she liked him as ell. Really liked him. And liking him as well as fancying im was the sort of dangerously lethal combination that could asily erode her resistance if she wasn't careful.

And that was why she'd spent the whole day dithering over hether to come this evening. Why she'd been pacing around er flat, frowning at the floor as she tried to work out what was going on inside her head, and what she was going to do bout it.

In the end, unable to figure anything sensible out and with arely half an hour before the launch started, she'd told herself stop being such a wimp and had pulled herself together.

So she might have to fortify her resistance and strengthen er resolve, but how could she not have come? For one thing he'd been working on this to the exclusion of all else, and was desperate to see the results of three weeks of hard slog. or another, she was longing to know if they'd got away with .

Besides, it was her birthday and she hadn't come up with nything else to do, and despite her previous determination to ury herself beneath her duvet and forget about it, she hadn't eally wanted to do that. At least not when there'd been the

chance to see Will one last time before their association cam
to an end.

So she'd whirled round her flat like a dervish, taking
shower, doing her hair, slapping on some make-up and throw
ing on a dress and shoes, and now here she was. Leaning ove
a display case that contained two of the pieces she'd restore
champagne glass in hand, and trying not to respond to th
feel of the pair of gorgeous blue eyes that had been borin
into her back ever since she'd arrived five minutes ago.

'Happy birthday, Bells.'

Bella jumped, straightened and swung round to see Phoeb
standing beside her, a slight frown creasing her forehead an
her smile a little strained.

'Thank you,' she said and gave her a quick kiss on th
cheek, wondering what was up and hoping it wasn't anythin
to do with the wedding plans.

'You know,' said Phoebe, 'I was going to say that I'm gla
you're doing something on your birthday, but now I'm not s
sure. Now I think it might have been better if you'd holed u
in your flat and forgotten all about it like you said you wer
going to in your email.'

'And miss the chance to get all dolled up, drink champagn
and catch up with colleagues?' said Bella with a grin. 'I don
think so.'

'Well, as long as that's all you're planning on doing,' sai
Phoebe, folding her arms across her chest and arching a
eyebrow.

Huh? Bella blinked. 'What?'

'Don't give me that innocent blink thing.' Phoebe narrowe
her eyes. 'What's going on between you and Will?'

Uh-oh. Bella's heart lurched. 'What makes you thin
there's anything going on between me and Will?' she sai
cagily.

'I can tell.'

'How?' she asked, glancing over at him standing there
talking to Alex, and her breath catching all over again.

God, he was gorgeous. The breadth of his shoulders, the
lean powerful body clad in a dark suit, and the magnetic energy he radiated never failed to scramble her senses. The sheer
impact he made on her, the pull he seemed to exert over her,
which was even stronger now that she knew so much more
about him, was almost irresistible. 'We haven't even spoken.'

'You don't need to. I've been watching the two of you for
the last five minutes and you can't take your eyes off each
other.'

Bella bit her lip. That much was true. It was as if she had
some kind of built-in radar where Will was concerned. The
minute she'd arrived her gaze had instantly zoomed in on
him and ever since she'd been aware of where he was, just
as she'd been achingly aware that he'd been watching her.

But he hadn't come over to say hello, and something about
the set of his jaw, and the dark expression on his face, made
her wary of going up to him. Given the circumstances of their
association, she figured, distance was probably for the best.

'You're circling each other like sharks,' Phoebe said,
frowning in consternation. 'Please, please, *please* tell me
you're not thinking what I think you're thinking.'

'OK,' said Bella, nodding slowly and sliding her gaze back
to her friend, 'I'm not thinking what you think I'm thinking.'
In fact she wasn't sure quite what she was thinking.

Phoebe let out a little wail and Bella had the impression
had she not been wearing three inch heels she'd have stamped
her foot. 'Oh, I knew it. I just *knew* it. What a complete and
utter mess. I could have killed Alex when he told me he'd
given Will your number.'

Bella blinked. 'Why?'

'Because I knew he'd fancy you. And vice versa. Why do

you think I haven't introduced you before? Will is *no* goo[c]
for you.'

'I think he might be very good for me.'

She'd meant it as a throwaway comment, but the minu[t]
the words left her lips her heart began to hammer and sh[e]
realised it was true. She might have managed to deny it f[o]
the last three interminable weeks, but she couldn't any lo[n]
ger. She wanted him. Badly. She was so desperate with th[e]
need to finish what they'd started on the back seat of his c[a]
that she thought she might die with the ache of it.

So Will wouldn't be any good for her in the long-ter[m]
but a part of her was beginning not to care. This foolhard[y]
reckless and increasingly insistent part of her was wonderi[n]
whether she wasn't being a bit melodramatic about the who[l]
thing. Wondering whether she shouldn't sling her long-ter[m]
aims to one side, give in and go for a short hot fling. It did[n]
have to detract from her long-term goals, did it? And beside[s]
it was her birthday. Didn't she deserve a little fun?

'No,' said Phoebe fiercely. 'He wouldn't. He'd be disas[s]
trous. Yes, he might be the most gorgeous man—after Ale[x]
of course—to walk the planet, but he doesn't do long-ter[m]
and he definitely doesn't do commitment.'

'I know.'

Phoebe went still and her eyebrows shot up. 'You do[.]
But...' Her face fell. 'Oh, God. I'm too late, aren't I?'

'I'm afraid so.'

'But he only does flings.'

'Short and hot, I understand.'

'Yes, by all accounts, but—'

'Well, that's good, then,' said Bella, draining her glas[s]
and setting it down on a table, 'because that's exactly what [I]
want. An extremely short, extremely scorching fling.'

'You don't.'

'I do.' God, she really did.

'Bella, listen to me,' said Phoebe, sounding a little panicked. 'If Will ever let things go further than a handful of dates he'd leave a trail of broken hearts all over the place. He really isn't what you need. You're far better off with someone like Sam.'

Yes, he was and no, she wasn't, Bella thought dazedly, staring at Will over the rim of her glass and feeling her blood heat. 'Don't worry, Phoebs,' she murmured. 'I just feel like a little fun on my birthday, that's all.'

'So get a manicure. Buy yourself a new handbag.'

'I don't want a manicure, or a new handbag. I want an affair with Will.' Whether he still wanted an affair with her, of course, was anyone's guess. Not once over the last three weeks had he flirted with her. Yes, their conversations had been wide-ranging and kind of personal, but they'd also been platonic and light. But never mind. She'd persuade him of the wisdom of her decision. How could she fail with such zeal on her side?

'You're mad.'

'Possibly.'

'Do you have any idea how catastrophic it could turn out to be?'

'It'll be fine. I'll be fine. He's not going to break my heart.'

'He will.'

'He won't. You said yourself he doesn't let it go that far. And neither will I.'

'But you may not have a lot of choice.'

She had every choice. And she'd made hers. It was simply a question of self-control and not letting her ultimate goal slip from her mind.

'Phoebe,' she said, shooting her friend a firm look, 'I appreciate your concern, really I do. But I've made up my mind and nothing you say will make any difference.'

Phoebe sighed, threw her hands up and gave in. 'Well, on

your head be it. But don't make the mistake of thinking you'l
be able to change him.'

'I wouldn't dream of it, and, in any case, I'm not sure I'e
want to.'

'That's what they all say,' said Phoebe darkly.

'Ah,' said Bella with a smile as her heart thumped, 'bu
the difference is, *I* mean it.'

'They all say that too.'

From the shadows Will watched Bella deep in conversatior
with Phoebe, and wondered when exactly he'd lost his mind

In theory, his plan to wear her resistance down had beer
perfect. Faultless, even, and utterly beautiful in its simplicity
All it had taken was one quick phone call when he'd returnec
home from the restaurant all those weeks ago, and that hac
been it.

At the time, he'd ignored the little voice inside his heac
insisting that the stake he was gambling with was too high
Just as he'd ignored the stab of guilt at laying the blame a
Caroline's door. As far as he'd been concerned the end woulc
justify the means.

Not only had his strategy given him the ideal opportunity
to stay in touch with Bella and embark on his war of attrition
it had also solved the problem of what to do about the dodgy
jewellery. Plus, as he received emails or phone calls pretty
much every week with a request to exhibit the collection, i
had been the ideal way to get people like the director of the
Grayson Museum off his back.

That his plan might have failed, might still fail, didn'
cross his mind. For one thing he didn't fail. Ever. For anothe
Bella was a perfectionist and he'd been certain she took fa
too much pride in her work to allow the finished result to be
anything other than flawless.

And OK, there had been that brief moment when he'd go

to her flat that Sunday morning and been hit by such a strong bolt of desire that he'd wanted to scoop her up in his arms and demand to know the location of her bedroom, which had definitely not been part of the plan. Neither had the surge of white-hot jealous fury when he thought she'd gone round to Sam's nor the relief when he realised she hadn't, or the overwhelming urge to gather her in his arms and kiss the life out of her just before he'd left.

But by and large things had gone exactly as he'd intended.

So why, over the course of the last week or so, had he found himself doubting the wisdom of his strategy? Where had the feeling that things weren't quite right sprung from? And what was the thing that had been stabbing at his conscience for the past few days?

Surely it couldn't be guilt, could it?

Will rubbed his chest and frowned. But what else could it be, when it had appeared right after she'd told him how much she valued honesty, annoyingly hammering home the point that he'd been less than truthful with her? Why else had he stopped dropping by her shop when previously he'd gone there almost every day?

He stifled a sigh. Yup. That definitely sounded like guilt. And it was probably guilt too that was preventing him from going over to her and saying hello.

Now his conscience had been roused it wasn't holding back, and questions and doubts began to attack him from all sides. What on earth gave him the right to persuade Bella into having an affair with him anyway? She'd said she didn't want one so he ought to respect that. Since when had he started disregarding other people's wishes in favour of his own?

And as for attrition, what had he been thinking? When exactly had his common sense, his integrity—such as it was— deserted him?

He glanced over at her, met her eyes head on, caught the

expression on her face and his entire body tightened with need. Well, his body could forget it because he was rapidly coming to the conclusion that an affair with Bella was the worst idea he'd ever had.

And actually not simply because he was being battered by a guilty conscience. When he'd set out on his attrition mission he'd never intended to get so personal. He'd planned to go easy on the chat and heavy on the innuendo. To bombard her with smouldering smiles and gratuitous touches and seduce her into his bed.

So what had happened? When exactly had things changed? How had he ended up telling her all about his life and his plans for the dukedom? And when exactly had he started liking her as well as wanting her?

Liking her—and so much—hadn't been factored into his plan. Nor had the notion that he might be more susceptible to her charms than he'd envisaged.

That his plan hadn't been quite so perfect left him feeling oddly unsettled. As did the dawning realisation that if he let things go any further he could well be at some sort of risk. What if she wasn't the only one who could be hurt by an affair? What if *he* got in too deep and couldn't get out?

As a bolt of alarm shot through him Will ran a finger around the inside of his collar, feeling as if it were strangling him. God, that really didn't bear thinking about. Never mind that it hadn't happened before. He wasn't naive enough to think that it couldn't happen eventually. It was just lucky he'd caught it early enough to think about throwing up some defences.

Which, he thought as he watched Bella heading towards him, were undoubtedly about to come in extremely useful. Because she wasn't just heading. She was sidling, only pausing to pluck a glass of champagne off a tray, a sexy smile curving her lips and a determined look in her eye. Something

out the way she moved had all the tiny hairs at the back
his neck leaping up in alarm. Every instinct he possessed
led at him to get as far away from her as he could. And
would have done exactly that had his feet not appeared to
ve taken root.

'Hi,' she said, coming to a standstill far too close for his
mfort and sending a thousand shivers scurrying over his
in.

Will fought the instinct to take a step back and shoved
s hands in his pockets instead. 'Hi,' he said, his voice a lot
lmer than he felt. 'You look spectacular.'

That was a bit of an understatement. In a short, tight, shim-
ering coppery dress that brought out the highlights in the
ir that was tumbling over her shoulders, and with the end-
ss legs, she looked good enough to eat.

'Thank you.' She ran her gaze over him and a thick slug-
sh heat began to seep along his veins. 'So do you.'

'Thank you.'

'So what's the verdict?' she asked, glancing up at him from
neath her eyelashes.

About what? The sudden awakening of his conscience? Her
ess and the clamouring urge he had to take her outside and
t her out of it? His slow inexorable descent into insanity?
bout what?'

'The evening. Do you think we've got away with it?'

'It certainly looks like it,' he said. 'Everyone seems awe-
ruck. Eyebrows are shooting up and mouths are dropping
en all over the place. I've never seen or heard anything like

'No?' she said, flashing him a wicked smile and tilting her
ad. 'Happens to me all the time.'

His heart lurched and his mouth went dry. What the hell
as going on? Was she flirting with him? 'I'm sure it does,'
murmured, narrowing his eyes as if that would somehow

lessen the destructive effect she was having on his newly d
covered principles.

'And what do *you* think?'

Will could barely breathe let alone think. 'I think we'
been incredibly lucky and it's an experience I never want
repeat,' he said, and he wasn't just referring to this evenin

'Pity,' she said, lifting the glass to her mouth and pressi
the rim against her lower lip. 'I've found it fun.'

And perhaps she wasn't either, he thought, his mouth dr
ing as she tilted the glass and parted her lips and gave him
glimpse of her tongue. Then she dropped her head back, gi
ing him a glorious view of her neck, and took a long swallc
of champagne. As she brought her head back up she dart
her tongue out to catch a drop of liquid that clung to her low
lip and let it linger before sweeping it along a bit. Will's ga
automatically dipped to trace the movement and his mir
went fuzzy. And then went even fuzzier at the light shinir
in the depths of her eyes.

'You've done an incredible job,' he said, barely able
speak.

'It's been an absolute pleasure.'

God. Had her gaze just darted to his groin? Whether he
been imagining things or not, the job that immediately sprar
into Will's mind was not of the professional kind. 'I'm gl
you think so.'

'Did you know today's my birthday?'

Will blinked and rubbed his jaw. 'I didn't. Happy birt
day.'

'I certainly hope it will be.'

She shot him another smouldering glance and Will felt h
skin prickle. 'Did you get anything nice?'

'My mother sent me an arnica plant.'

'Why?'

'I have absolutely no idea. Still, it could have been worse.
t one point she asked me if I'd like a goat.'

'Not hugely convenient.'

'No.' Bella shuddered and Will tried not to notice the way
er body moved. 'Imagine the mess.'

'And the noise.'

'Well, quite.' She paused. 'You know what I'd really like?'

His body tightened at the drop in her voice. 'I can't imag-
ie,' he murmured.

'Can't you?'

She shot him a scorching look from beneath her lashes and
Vill gritted his teeth. What was going on here? How was he
o maintain his principled stance when she was in this foxy
rame of mind? And why was she in this foxy frame of mind
nyway? As bewilderment and frustration spun through him
Vill had finally had enough. 'What are you doing, Bella?'

She smiled up at him and arched an eyebrow. 'Toying with
ie idea of seducing you.'

For a moment Will thought he must have misheard. But
ie punch of desire that struck him in the stomach and robbed
im of breath told him he hadn't. Dammit, why couldn't she
ave done all this *before* he'd decided he couldn't pursue an
ffair with her? Say, when he'd first suggested it back at that
estaurant. Her timing really was abysmal. 'I see.'

'If I decided to go through with it, would I succeed?'

God, probably. Will curled his hands into fists, set his jaw
nd reminded himself of all the excellent reasons why she
vouldn't. 'No.'

'OK,' she said, nodding slowly and batting her eyelashes
p at him. 'I guess I could let you seduce me if you'd prefer.'

His entire body tensed. 'Definitely not.'

Her smile faltered a little. 'Oh. Right…' She bit her lip and
rowned. 'Why not?'

'It wouldn't be right.'

For a moment Bella simply stared at him. 'Scruples, Will'

'Looks like it, doesn't it?'

She blinked. 'But why? I want you. I think you want me
So what's the problem?'

He did want her. Oh, how he wanted her... 'I'm not th
man you seem to think I am.'

Bella gave her head a quick shake and then smiled. 'O
dear,' she said softly. 'First Phoebe, now you.'

'What?'

'Phoebe warned me off you.'

Will fought down the stab of irritation that that aroused
'She was right to do so.'

'Surely you can't be that bad?'

Judging by the light sparkling in the depths of her eye
Bella was clearly hoping that he was as bad as could be.

Time to disillusion her.

Taking in a quick sharp breath, Will drew himself up t
his full height and looked down at her. 'I lied, Bella.'

Her eyes widened. 'About what?'

'This evening.'

She tilted her head and looked up at him and Will felt as i
she could see right into the depths of his soul. 'In what way?

'It was my idea. The whole thing.' He pulled his hands ou
of his pockets and waved them in the direction of the displa
cases before raking them through his hair and then shovin
them back in his pockets. 'Caroline didn't promise the col
lection to anyone.'

'She didn't?'

He shook his head, his eyes blazing into hers as he trie
to make her see. 'I did. *I* was the one who rang the directo
of the museum. *I* was the one who told him he could exhibi
it.'

She frowned and he felt something like regret lodge in hi
chest. 'Why?'

'Attrition.'

'What?'

'Attrition. Erosion by friction.'

'Yes, I'm aware of what it is,' she said. 'But what does it have to do with anything?'

'Everything,' he said abruptly. 'I've spent the last three weeks wanting to wear you down.'

'I see.' She paused. Pondered his words for a second. 'And why would you want to wear me down?'

'To get you to see things from my point of view.' Even as he said it he felt like a heel, and shame rolled around inside him. 'To persuade you to have an affair with me. You were so determined to deny the chemistry between us, it wound me up.'

She gave him a sexy little smile, took a step closer and put a hand on his chest. Every one of his senses was filled with her and a tremor went through him. 'Games, Will?'

A muscle hammered in his jaw and he curled his hands into fists. 'Perhaps.'

'I see… Was the whole thing a set-up? Right from the start?'

'God, no. Just this evening. I swear.'

She shot him a sultry smile and moved her hand down his chest and around to his back. 'Good. Then that's OK.'

Will was so bewitched by the feel of her hand idly stroking his back that at first he didn't register what she'd said. And then it filtered into his head and he made himself focus. OK? Didn't she care that he'd lied? What about the honesty she'd said she was so keen on? 'Don't you mind?'

'Not particularly. Actually I'm rather flattered that you'd go to such lengths to get me into bed.' She grinned. 'And it's worked, hasn't it? I do want to have an affair with you.'

'It's not going to happen.' Her hand could stop that. In fact he ought to remove it. And he would. In a minute.

'Hmm. Now who's the one denying the chemistry?'

'I don't deny it. I'm simply not going to do anything about it.'

'Why not?'

A muscle ticced in his jaw. 'You were right. I'd only hurt you.' Not to mention what she could do to him. Was already doing to him just by putting her hand on him.

She tilted her head and regarded him for so long that Will's insides began to curdle. 'I appreciate you're trying to be noble,' she said, 'but don't you think that's for me to decide?'

Will tensed. 'I'm not going to change, Bella.'

'I know that. I don't want you to. And neither am I. All I want is a quick fling.'

He frowned. His heart thumped. A quick fling? Was she for real? 'No, you don't.'

Bella let out a frustrated sigh and withdrew her hand to fold her arms over her chest. 'I'm getting a bit fed up with people telling me what I want. Look, I've thought it through, at length, and I want an affair. With you. Assuming you're up for it, of course.'

Oh, he was up for it. More than up for it. So up for it in fact that he was in agony. And just like that his paltry defences, the ones that he hadn't yet had the time to fortify, crumbled.

An affair didn't have to hurt anyone, did it? Bella seemed to know what she wanted, and if she'd really thought it through as she claimed then he ought to respect that. She wasn't stupid; she was perfectly aware of what an affair with him would be about.

And as for him, well, he'd had affairs before. Plenty of them in the last few years. And not once had he got his fingers burnt. So why did it need to be any different with Bella? As long as he kept his head, stuck to electrifying sex and avoided any kind of personal conversation, he'd be fine. They both would be.

'And then what?' he murmured as the possibility of an affair with Bella heated his blood and sent desire ricocheting around him.

'We go our separate ways.' She tilted her head. 'I haven't changed what I want,' she said, 'and I'm not going to. I still want to get married. I still want security and stability. However, in the absence of any progress on that front, I feel like some fun. Hot temporary fun. Do you object?'

Object? He could hardly think straight. 'How could I possibly object?' he said hoarsely.

'Good.' Bella grinned. 'So…do you need to stick around any longer?'

And continue to suffer from aching frustration as well as having to muster up some kind of response to all the platitudes he'd received about how great it was that the collection was finally on display and what a wonderful commemoration of his father's life it was? No way. 'No.'

Bella gave him a slow smile and her eyes shimmered. 'Then I'll go and get my coat, shall I?'

CHAPTER ELEVEN

WELL, thank God for that, thought Bella, sitting on the back seat of the car, her heart thundering and her body pulsating with desire.

For a moment back there, in the dark shadows of the museum, she'd truly thought it wasn't going to happen. That Will would stick to what he'd decided was the right thing to do, and continue to deny the attraction she'd been able to tell he still felt.

But luckily for her, wherever that sudden attack of the scruples had sprung from it had sprung right back, and they were now speeding away from the museum, through the dark streets of London and heading towards a night that she was aching for. Had been aching for for quite some time, if she was being honest.

As a result of her conversational success her whole body was now trembling with need and anticipation, and her head was throbbing. She cast a quick glance at Will and caught her breath. He was sitting back and staring straight ahead, utterly still, the tension and tightly restrained desire rolling off him in great waves.

At the thought of having all that desire unleashed on her, Bella couldn't stand it any longer. Why wait until they got to a bed? What was wrong with here? Now?

Her heart banging against her ribs, she leaned forwards to

press the button that would raise the partition between them and Bob, and prepared to launch herself at him.

But nothing happened. So she pressed it again. It gave a clunk and she let out a groan of frustration.

'It's bust.' Will's voice was tight.

'Damn,' Bella murmured.

'If it wasn't,' he said, twisting round to look at her, his eyes dark and blazing with heat and promise, 'do you really think you would still be sitting there upright and fully clothed?'

Her mouth went dry and she swallowed as lust belted around her insides. 'I guess not. You should get Bob to fix it.'

'I will.'

After that, conversation seemed pointless so Bella sat on her hands and crossed her legs at her ankles and pressed her thighs together in an attempt to stop the throbbing between them. But it didn't work. The pressure only made things worse.

After what felt like an eternity, the car slowed and barely before it had stopped Will was out, whipping round to her side, opening her door and practically dragging her to her feet. Gritting out a rough goodnight to Bob, he led Bella up the steps, thrust the key into the lock and opened the front door.

Bella didn't have time to notice the elegance of the house because the minute the door slammed behind them Will was pinning her up against it with his body, planting his hands on either side of her head as his mouth crashed down on hers.

She moaned and threw her arms around his neck and tilted her hips to grind against him, the desperation to have him hard and deep inside her almost too painful to bear. The kiss deepened, spun out of control and then they were groaning and panting and grappling at clothing.

Bella thrust her hands beneath the lapels of Will's jacket and off it came, dropping to the marble floor, along with his coat. He eased her out of hers and then his hands were shooting down to the hem of her dress and bunching it up while her hands fumbled with his belt.

And then just when she thought that finally, *finally*, she'd have him inside her, Will broke off and jerked back, his breathing ragged and his face dark. 'Wait,' he muttered.

Wait? *Wait?* Bella's heart thumped and a shiver ran down her spine. What on earth did he want to wait for? Hadn't they waited long enough? Surely he couldn't be having *another* attack of the scruples? 'Why?' she said hoarsely.

'Not here,' he muttered, taking her hand and pulling her along the dark shadowy hall towards the stairs. 'This time I want you horizontal. And naked.'

Oh, thank God, she thought, relief pouring through her as she twined her fingers tightly with his and followed. That was fair enough. She wanted him horizontal and naked too.

It took a while to get to his bedroom. Every five seconds Will would stop and either bend her over the banister or press her against the wall to give her hot kisses that melted her bones. His hands didn't leave her, and by the time he backed her into his bedroom she was shaking with such desire that her knees were about to give way.

He kicked the door shut and then his fingers found the side zip of her dress and slid it down. The silk pooled in a heap at her feet and Bella stepped out of it, standing in front of him in nothing but a strapless bra, knickers, stockings and high heels.

She heard his sharp intake of breath, watched him swallow, and a surge of primitive female satisfaction darted through her.

Then he tumbled her back and she landed on the bed with a soft thud and as she watched Will kick off his shoes and strip off the rest of his clothes it was her turn to catch her breath.

God, he could really give Rodin's *Adam* a run for his

money in the hot bod department. Everywhere she looked he was tanned skin sprinkled with dark fine hairs, and lean hard muscle. Her eyes darted over his shoulders, his chest, and then down over his taut abdomen to his mouth-watering erection and her insides turned to molten heat.

Will lowered himself onto the bed beside her and Bella felt a delirious smile spread across her face. He rolled over her and as her arms went round his neck and his mouth came down on hers the uppermost thought in her head was that this was without doubt going to be the best birthday she'd ever had.

And then as their tongues met and his hand tangled in her hair she couldn't think about anything at all except the way he made her feel.

She bent her leg and hooked it round his to pull him closer and tilted her pelvis so she could feel the tip of his erection press against the sensitive nub of her clitoris.

She heard him groan, and shuddered. Desire pounded in the pit of her stomach as she ran her hands over the muscles of his back, taking her time, caressing and marvelling at his heat and the tightening of his skin wherever her fingers trailed.

Will drew back, and stared down at her, his eyes glittering and fathomless. 'You know, you really are going to kill me,' he muttered, winding a hand beneath her to unclip her bra.

Bella arched her back to help him. 'The feeling is entirely mutual,' she breathed as he removed her bra and tossed it aside.

His gaze dipped to her mouth and, even though they'd been kissing only a second ago, her lips tingled and ached and every inch of her was desperate to feel his mouth on hers again. 'Did I mention I looked up belladonna on the internet the other day?' he murmured, setting his mouth to her neck and cupping her breast with the hand that wasn't taking his weight.

Bella's breath hitched in her throat. 'And?'

'Apparently among its side effects are minor visual distortions, an inability to focus on near objects and an increased heart rate.'

'Interesting,' she said, wondering how much longer she was going to be expected to contribute to this conversation, because with the way her brain was disintegrating a couple of seconds was all she had left.

'I thought so. Especially since I appear to be suffering from all of them.'

'Oh, dear.'

'Know of an antidote?'

'Abstinence?'

He pressed his mouth to the pulse hammering at the base of her neck and Bella bit her lip. 'Really not an option at the moment,' he murmured.

'Inoculation, then?'

He gave her a smile that had her stomach quivering and then bent his head to her breast and flicked his tongue over her nipple and Bella moaned. 'That sounds more like it,' he murmured, shifting lower, his mouth moving, hot and wet, over the skin of her stomach.

With every inch of her feeling as if it were on fire, Bella couldn't prevent a whimper escaping her lips as he hooked his thumbs over the top of her knickers and slid them, her suspender belt and her stockings down her legs. He dispensed with her shoes and finally she was as naked and as horizontal as he was.

And then she felt the touch of his mouth against the molten burning centre of her, and nearly jackknifed off the bed. Her heart hammered as sparks of ecstasy began to shoot through her.

Bella squirmed as her head swam and then when Will planted his hands on her hips, anchoring her to the mattress and keeping her where he wanted her, she let her eyelids flutter closed and gave herself up to the pleasure. Because, God, he was good at this.

Her hands flexed against the sheets and then dug into his hair and she had to bite on her lip to stop herself screaming as the pressure inside her started to build. Her head dropped back, her knees fell open wider and as he delved deeper, harder, his tongue stroking faster and faster over her clitoris, Bella couldn't take it any more.

Everything inside her tightened into a tight ball of tension and then shattered. Her back arched. Her breath caught. And then she was spinning off into a whirlpool of bliss, the waves of pleasure rolling over her so hard and so fast that she thought she might drown in the sensation.

As the tremors racking her body faded and her breathing and pulse regulated Will kissed his way back up her body until he was lying on top of her and pressing her to the bed. At the desire blazing in his eyes, Bella's heart rate picked up all over again.

'Happy birthday?' he murmured.

'What do you think?' she said, giving him a lazy sated smile. 'As presents go that was *much* better than an arnica plant.'

Will frowned and propped himself up on his elbows. 'Are you comparing me to a plant?'

Bella grinned at the look of pique on his face. 'Very possibly.'

'I think I'm devastated.'

She leaned up and pressed a quick kiss on his mouth. 'I'm sorry.'

Will shook his head in mock regret. 'It's way too late for an apology. I think my ego might be bruised beyond belief.'

Bella grinned again. 'Then I recommend you take arnica. It's good for bruises.'

His eyes glinted with a deliciously wicked gleam. 'I'll bear it in mind. Although right now I think I'd rather take you.'

She lifted her arms above her head, stretched against him and shot him a smouldering smile. 'Oh, well, in that case I'm all yours.' She batted her eyelids up at him. 'Feel free to do whatever you want with me.'

For a moment he just stared down at her, and then, as if struck with a cattle prod, Will was rolling off her, grabbing a condom from the drawer of the bedside table and ripping it open with his teeth. Her heart thudding madly, she bent her knees, opened her legs, and then he was sheathing himself, moving between her legs and surging forwards and entering and filling her in one smooth powerful thrust.

Bella let out a rough groan and wrapped her arms around his back and her legs around his waist, and clung on for dear life as he captured her mouth with his.

And then he began to move inside her. Slowly, rhythmically and smoothly, and maddeningly in control.

Which would have been amazing, devastating even, if she'd wanted slow smooth and control. But she didn't. She wanted fast and frantic and furious. She writhed against him, but it got her nowhere. He was the one setting the pace. He was the one in control, as if he somehow needed to prove that this was controllable, and it was driving her nuts.

Desperation clawed at her insides and she dragged her mouth away from his. 'I never did tell you what I really wanted for my birthday, did I?' she said, her voice sounding thick and rough and heavy with desire.

Will went still. 'No,' he muttered, his jaw tight with the effort of holding onto that infernal control of his. 'You didn't.'

'Would you like to know?'

'Now?'

'It's relevant, believe me.'

'Fine.'

She planted a hand on the back of his neck, lifted her head and whispered in his ear. A few short words. Highly descriptive. Highly explicit. Leaving him in no doubt whatsoever about what she wanted from him right now.

She drew back and looked into his eyes and saw that her words had had exactly the effect she'd hoped for. Gone was the infuriatingly rigid control. Gone was any memory of slow and smooth. Instead she saw nothing but raw, naked need in his glittering gaze.

Bella arched an eyebrow, gave him the hint of a suggestive smile, and then with a low growl Will was pulling out of her, flipping her over, gripping her hips and then plunging back inside her so hard, so deep that she nearly climaxed right then and there.

She leant on her elbows and pushed back against him, going completely mindless as he drove into her and hit her G-spot over and over again while trailing kisses up and down her spine.

Her blood pounded in her ears, her heart thundered, and pleasure and heat coiled low in her stomach. Will snaked one arm around her, pressed his hand against her and stroked her clitoris, and her breathing quickened.

He leaned over her, murmuring how good she felt, telling her exactly what she was doing to him, and his voice, so hoarse and rough, scraped over her nerve endings, ratcheting up the delicious tension coiling deep inside her.

And then he was sitting back, taking her with him, pulling her tight against him and slamming into her as deep and as hard as he could, and without warning Bella splintered. As pleasure exploded though her, shooting through her veins, making her shudder and tremble and whimper, Will wrapped his arms around her, and she heard him groan, felt him tense and pulsate deep inside her as she clenched and squeezed and quivered around him.

She could feel his heart hammering against her back, feel the heat of his body seeping into hers and as her trembling subsided she relaxed against him and tried to keep the wide smile off her face. But it was hard not to grin when he was stroking her breast, rubbing his thumb over her nipple and kissing his way along her shoulder to her neck. Feeling deliciously wanton and languid, Bella shuddered and felt him twitch deep inside her in response.

'So that was what I wanted,' she murmured as evenly as she could, eventually easing herself off him and twisting round to kiss him on the mouth. 'Now why don't you tell me what *you'd* like for *your* birthday?'

She took care of the condom and pushed him back so that she could lie flat on top of him. With a soft 'Oof' Will landed on the pillows and slid his arms round her. 'My birthday isn't until March,' he said, giving her a faint smile as he ran his fingers lightly up and down her back. 'And I wasn't exactly doing you a favour.'

She tilted her head and determinedly didn't think about how there'd be no more of this come March. 'Then perhaps there's something I could do to apologise for comparing you to a plant.'

A flicker leapt in the depths of his eyes and she felt him stirring against her thigh. 'Well, if you absolutely insist.'

'I do.' She nodded. 'I'm all for equality.'

'What did you have in mind?'

Giving him a wide smile, Bella arched an eyebrow and began to slide her way down his body. 'If you really can't think of anything, I'll be forced to take matters into my own hands.'

She wrapped her fingers around his growing erection and Will blew out a long shuddering breath. 'That's absolutely fine with me.'

So much for attrition, thought Will some time later, his eyes closed as he listened to the soft sound of Bella's breathing.

There he'd been, confident he was in the driving seat, that he was in control, when she'd whispered what she'd like him to do to her, and all control had vanished. His mind had gone completely blank and all that had remained was the primitive all-consuming need to possess her.

So who exactly had worn down whom?

Not that it mattered any more. Over the course of the past couple of hours they'd worn each other down—and out—in a highly satisfactory manner, and he was back to thinking that an affair with Bella was the best idea he'd ever had and thanking God that she'd managed to change his mind.

'I think we should establish some sort of boundaries, don't you?'

Bella's husky voice cut across Will's musings and he opened one eye and glanced down at her, his eyebrows snapping together in a frown.

Hmm. Boundaries. Good point. Slightly strange that it had been brought up by her when he was always the one to dictate the terms of his affairs, generally before they'd even started, but never mind. Whoever had brought it up was irrelevant. Establishing boundaries was the priority and he rather thought he'd be interested to see what she came up with. A novel approach for him, perhaps, but then everything about his dealings with Bella was novel.

'What do you suggest?'

She caught her lip and hmmed. 'A time limit would be good. At the very least.'

Ah, his favourite kind of boundary. 'What were you thinking?'

'Well, I don't know really... How long is the collection on display?'

'A month.'

'Great. Then how about we stop when it does?'

Will twirled a lock of her hair around his finger and watched it change colour in the dim light as he contemplated her proposal.

A month ought to be fine. It was longer than some of his affairs, not as long as others. Perfectly reasonable, and would give him plenty of time to satisfy his craving for her. 'That sounds sensible.'

'Of course if either of us wants to get out before then, maybe if you get bored or something, then we can stop.'

Will felt his eyebrows shoot up. 'You really think I might get bored?' That didn't seem likely from where he was lying.

She smiled up at him. 'It could happen.'

He rolled her over, his body tightening as he stared down at her and lowered his head. 'Then we'll just have to get inventive, won't we?'

CHAPTER TWELVE

BELLA was about to get very inventive indeed.

But not because she was bored. Far from it. She and Will had been seeing each other every night for the last fortnight. Some lunchtimes too, and she was loving every minute of it. Deciding to have an affair with Will was without doubt the best idea she'd ever had.

They'd been out for dinners and met up for walks in the park. They'd stayed in and she'd cooked. Last week he'd dropped by her shop. He hadn't even said hello, had just flicked the sign on the door to closed, then fixed her with a gaze that had her heart thundering, taken her hand and pulled her into the workshop at the back. He'd lifted her onto her workbench, bunched her dress up and given her the quickest, hottest sexual experience of her life. When she'd finally managed to get her breath back, she'd dragged him up to her flat and they'd spent the rest of the afternoon there, testing out the strength of various pieces of her furniture and discovering that while her sofa was sturdy, the bar stools in her kitchen were less so.

So she was far from bored.

No. The reason she was marching through Soho, heading in the direction of a very specific shop, was while the sex was fabulous and more thrilling than she could ever have imagined, Will's reluctance to talk about himself, the reasons for his aversion to commitment in particular, was driving her nuts.

On the rare occasions she had broached the subject, or any subject of a personal nature for that matter, he'd employed more effective countermeasures than an intercontinental ballistic missile. If they were out, he'd shoot her a dazzling smile that scrambled her brain to such an extent that she forgot what she'd been asking. If they were in he'd give her a look that had her horizontal and writhing beneath him within seconds.

She'd tried to work it out for herself but had drawn a blank. That something had caused it was obvious. It was all very well not wanting to be tied down at the age of, say, twenty-one, but to be single at thirty-six, when Will was gorgeous and intelligent and sometimes really quite funny, simply wasn't normal. Under normal circumstances he'd have been snapped up years ago.

But what was at the root of it remained a mystery. He was as reluctant to chat now as he'd been keen to before the launch party, and that she found strange.

Arriving at the shop and pushing the door open, Bella reminded herself yet again that it shouldn't matter. Their fling was temporary so she had no need to know why Will was so averse to commitment. But knowing that she had no need to know anything that personal about him didn't stop her *wanting* to know. It didn't stop her wanting to know what made him the man he was. What had caused the shadows in his eyes that she caught glimpses of from time to time.

Wanting to know everything about him, in fact.

Her heart stumbled and she jerked to a halt in front of a display stand. She frowned while her head swam. Uh-oh. That didn't sound too good. That sounded kind of dangerous. Emotionally dangerous.

And then she pulled herself together and told herself not to be so absurd. She wasn't in any danger, emotionally or otherwise. She hadn't lost track of what she ultimately wanted. And she hadn't fallen into the trap of hoping that Will might be able to provide it, or that, despite her assurances to Phoebe to the contrary, she might be able to change him.

No, she thought, eyeing up the racks of merchandise as heat began to race through her veins and desire hummed in the pit of her stomach. It was curiosity. Simple as that. And as she was pretty sure Will was never going to tell her what she wanted to know of his own accord, she was going to torment him into talking.

It was just as well he had a reliable capable team running his business over in the Cayman Islands, thought Will, striding along the pavement towards Bella's shop, his body tight with anticipation and desire pounding through him. Because if it had been solely down to him, he'd be heading for bankruptcy.

Work? What a joke. Since their affair had started he'd barely been able to focus on anything other than Bella and when he'd next be seeing her. She was amazing. Insatiable. Utterly intoxicating, and he couldn't seem to get enough of her. She had him thinking about things he couldn't have and behaving totally out of character.

Why else would he have ditched the meeting he was supposed to be having in response to her phone call an hour ago? Why else would his body have leapt to attention when she'd suggested he meet her here in half an hour? Why else would he have made himself sit on his chair and coolly tell her to make it an hour when every cell of his body urged him to make it five minutes? What on earth had he been trying to prove by doing that? That he did in fact have some sort of masochistic streak? That he was in some sort of control over this?

Will stopped at her front door and pressed the buzzer. That was even more of a joke. He'd lost control over this the minute she'd stared up at him at the museum and told him she wanted an affair with him.

Which could well be why the idea of her not being around for his birthday in March was beginning to feel distinctly unappealing. Why he was beginning to get the feeling that at the end of the month he might not be able to let her go.

Will froze as something punched him in the stomach. His heart skipped a beat. And then he gave himself a quick shake and forced himself to relax.

Not be able to let her go? That was ridiculous. Of course he'd be able to let her go. Because that was the agreement. That was what they both wanted. And basically because he didn't have any choice. And come March he'd be…well, who knew where he'd be? But wherever he was Bella definitely wouldn't be with him.

Whatever was going on in his poor perplexed brain, one thing was clear. They only had another two weeks and he intended to make the most of every minute.

'Come on up.'

Starting now. Her voice, lower and more sultry than he remembered from this morning, had lust pounding through him so hard and so fast that all thoughts of where Bella might be in March vanished. All he was interested in was where she was right now.

He pushed the door open and attacked the stairs two at a time. He got to the top to find the door to her flat ajar and for some reason his pulse began to race.

'Bella?' he said, stepping over her threshold, shrugging out of his coat and dropping it on the chair.

'In here.'

Her voice came from the direction of her bedroom and Will strode along the passageway and threw open the door.

And nearly passed out. He stopped, his breath shooting

from his lungs and the bolt of lust thundering through him almost slammed him back against the wall.

Bella was lying on her bed, reclining against a bank of pillows and wearing nothing but a kind of black lacy corset, black stockings, black high heels and a very sultry smile.

All he could do was stare at her, desire punching him from the inside out, his mouth dry as his eyes roamed over her.

'Hi,' she said huskily, her eyes dark and inviting and promising things that made his stomach clench.

Will swallowed. Coughed. Wondered if he'd ever be able to speak again. 'Hi.' Hmm. Barely.

She rose off the bed and swung her legs to the floor and stood up. The corset pulled in her waist and made her breasts swell over the top. Her heels made her legs look endlessly long. She sidled over to him, her hips mesmerising him as they swayed from side to side.

Unable to take his eyes off her, Will couldn't move. His feet seemed to be glued to the floor. He clenched his hands into fists to stop himself from reaching for her and thrust them into the pockets of his jeans just to make sure. She'd clearly put a lot of thought into this seduction routine and who was he to spoil it?

'So how's your day been?' she said, standing right in front of him, placing her hands on his chest and planting a hot wet kiss on his mouth.

'Fine,' he said raggedly when she eventually drew back. 'Getting better by the second.'

'I do hope so.'

Glancing up at him from beneath her lashes, she gave him a smile that wiped his mind and then set about undoing the buttons of his shirt. As she slid his shirt from his shoulders, down his arms and off, she pressed a kiss to his chest, flicked her tongue over his nipple and Will shuddered.

Achingly slowly she unbuckled his belt and undid his jeans

and sank to her knees as she pushed them down his legs. He
hair brushed over his throbbing erection and he had to clasp
his hands behind his head to stop himself from burying his
hands in her hair and guiding her head and her mouth to
where he desperately wanted her.

His legs feeling weirdly weak, Will stepped out of his jean
and kicked off his shoes and then Bella was sliding her hands
over his calves and the backs of his thighs and he closed his
eyes in desperation.

Her breath whispered over his skin and then she was brushing her mouth up his thigh and over his erection and then
higher, across his stomach, his chest until she was standing
up and he was a moment away from dragging her to the floor
and burying himself inside her.

'Lie on the bed,' she murmured, her voice low and husky

'Bossy.'

'I'll make it worth your while, I promise.'

'In that case,' he drawled as a series of thrills raced through
him, 'why would I even want to try and argue?'

'Sensible man.'

God, he thought as he did as she'd ordered and watched
a satisfied smile curve her lips, he'd never felt less sensible

'What next?'

'Now put your hands behind your head.'

He did. 'What's got into you?' he said, deciding that whatever it was he liked it a lot.

'Nothing yet,' she purred, climbing on top of him and giving him a long slow kiss that blew his mind.

She kissed her way down his neck and along his collar-
bone, taking her time, making him burn up with need and he
had to fight to keep himself where he was.

A tremor racked his body and he marvelled that she could
do this to him. Thought that perhaps he should encourage her
to do it more often. Because there was definitely something

o be said for female dominance in the bedroom. Especially
with the way she was sliding her hands along his arms and
curling his fingers around the bars of her bed-head, giving
him an eyeful of soft pillowy cleavage.

His body tight with arousal and his heart thudding with
expectation, Will couldn't resist. He lifted his head and gently
nipped her flesh. She shuddered, then smiled seductively
down at him, slipping her hands beneath the pillows as she
wriggled on top of him.

He was contemplating undoing the strings of her corset
with his teeth, when out of the corner of his eye he caught a
flash of red fur, and before he knew it she'd surged up and
forwards and cuffed him to the bed.

There, thought Bella, feeling triumph roar through her as she
drew back and admired her handiwork. That hadn't been too
difficult, had it? Not when Will had been so pleasingly and
predictably cooperative.

Her plan had gone like clockwork and now she had him exactly where she wanted him. Naked. Exposed. Unable to take
control and distract her, and completely at her mercy. Once
she'd driven him demented with her hands and her mouth,
he'd be begging her for release and willing to tell her exactly
what his issue with commitment was.

Assuming she managed to hold out that long, of course.
She was so turned on by the sight of him lying there trapped
that part of her wanted to ditch her plan and simply straddle
him and sink herself down on him.

Hmm. There'd be plenty of time for that later, she told herself. Having spent so long firstly devising her plan, and then
umming and aahing over whether to go through with it, she
wasn't about to back out now.

'What the hell is this, Bella?' Will's voice was tight and
sharp and Bella suppressed the flicker of alarm that darted

through her. So he had a thing about control. That was tough.
Right now, so did she.

'I'd have thought it was perfectly obvious,' she said with
a smouldering smile.

'Unlock me,' he snapped.

'Soon.'

'Now.' His jaw clenched and his eyes blazed.

'No.' Where would she start? Should she work her way
from top to bottom and build up slowly? Or should she just
go straight for the sexual jugular, so to speak?

'Bella, get the bloody keys.'

'Too late,' she said silkily, drawing them from her cleavage and throwing them out of the window before turning her
attention back to the magnificence of Will's body. Whether
she lingered or hurried, she doubted he'd be the only one tor-
mented. Heat pummelled along her veins at the thought that
she could do anything with him she wanted, and her head
swam.

And then through the fog swilling around inside her head
she heard Will swear violently and she frowned, her gaze
snapping up to his face.

The flicker of alarm she'd managed to suppress a minute
ago flared into life. God. He looked utterly horrified.

Her heart lurched and her brain raced. During all her de-
liberations, she'd imagined he might have put up token resistance to being handcuffed to her bed-head, but she'd never
imagined he'd be quite so appalled.

But maybe it wasn't appal. Maybe it was something else.
Because actually, now she was looking at his face, she could
see that he'd gone so ghostly pale that if it hadn't been for his
tan he'd have been white. Sweat beaded on his forehead and
he was shaking. His muscles had tensed and his veins on his
arms and neck bulged. He looked as if he was in agony.

Oh, God, thought Bella, her heart hammering now with

eal panic. Perhaps this hadn't been such a good idea after ll. Perhaps she ought to release him. Right now.

Hastily she reached up and pulled a pin from her hair. She nbent it with her teeth and then leaned over him. She swiftly icked first one lock and then the other, and within a split econd he'd yanked his hands free, surged up and twisted ound so that Bella was flat on her back and he was looming ver her, his eyes wild and the pulse at the base of his neck hundering.

'You really shouldn't have done that,' he said roughly.

'I'm sorry,' she said, meaning it even as her heart pounded nd her breath caught in her throat.

'You will be.'

For a moment he hovered there, staring blindly down at er, his face tight and his body even tighter. But gradually he fierce blaze in his eyes ebbed, his expression relaxed and he colour returned to his face. Bella waited, not sure what o do or what to say. And then he dragged in a shaky breath, erked away and fell back on the bed.

Giving him a few moments to recover, she lifted herself p onto her elbows. 'So what was that all about?' she mur- nured once his breathing had regulated and she'd felt what- ever it was that had taken hold of him dissipate.

'Nothing.'

She rolled onto her side and looked at him closely. If he hought he could get away with brushing her off like that he ould think again. No way was she letting this lie. It was too ntriguing for words and she intended to get to the bottom of t whether he liked it or not. 'You're pale and you're shaking,' he said softly. 'That's not nothing.'

Will sighed and rubbed a hand over his face and forced imself to calm down. The terror and the nausea that had lammed into him the minute he'd realised what she'd done vere fading and it was fine. He was fine. But for a moment

there, when Bella had tossed the keys out of the window, he'
thought he'd been about to pass out. 'It's no big deal,' he mut
tered. 'I'm just not a huge fan of being locked up, that's all.

'Clearly. But why not?'

He set his jaw. 'Who is?'

'Plenty of people.'

'Well, I'm not one of them.'

She bit her lip and frowned, her gaze turning far too prob
ing for his comfort. Long seconds passed before she spok
again. 'You flinch every time you come into my shop, I'v
never seen you get into a lift and you'd rather walk than tak
a taxi.'

It was a statement rather than a question and Will felt to
sapped of energy to argue. Instead he avoided her eyes an
muttered, 'Yes, well, automatic locking mechanisms aren'
really my thing.'

'So what is it? Claustrophobia?'

He heard the curiosity in her voice and gritted his teeth
'Cleithrophobia actually, but it's not as bad as that. It's not
phobia. It's just a minor thing I have a slight problem with.'

'If you say so,' she said and he heard the hint of a smile i
her voice. 'What's cleithrophobia?'

'The fear of being locked in an enclosed space.' He sti
fled a shudder. '*I* don't particularly enjoy being locked in an
space, enclosed or otherwise.'

'I see. I'm sorry.'

'It's fine.'

Another few heartbeats of silence followed and Will won
dered if he could hope that that was it. But then she said, 'S
what happened?' and his stomach plummeted.

'What do you mean, what happened?' He tensed and stare
fixedly at the ceiling.

'Well, something must have caused it. In the first place,
mean.'

He closed his eyes as if somehow that might deter her from asking any more annoyingly persistent questions, and said vaguely, 'I don't really remember.'

Bella let out a soft 'you don't fool me' kind of a laugh and then pressed herself closer. 'Maybe I could help.'

'I doubt it.'

'Try me.'

Will opened his eyes and stared at her. 'Are you going to let this go?'

'I'd rather not, but I can't make you tell me if you don't want to.' She shot him a shrewd look. 'Of course your reluctance to talk about it could lead me to believe that it's not quite as trivial as you'd like me to think.'

Will narrowed his eyes at her. Perhaps she had a point. Irritatingly enough. And then he felt something inside him deflate. Oh, what the hell? If she was interested enough to want to know, then he'd tell her. What was such a big deal about it anyway? It wasn't as if it were *that* huge a part of his life.

'Fine,' he muttered. 'When I was a child I got stuck in a cupboard.'

'How?'

'The door swung shut behind me before I could stop it.'

'And it had one of those automatic locking mechanisms you're not too keen on?'

Feeling oddly cold, Will pulled the sheet over the lower half of his body. 'Exactly.'

Bella shifted closer and put her head on his shoulder and a hand on his chest. 'How horrible.'

'It wasn't particularly pleasant,' he murmured, deciding that understatement might well be the way to get through this. Understatement, sticking to the facts, ignoring how he'd felt at the time and concentrating on the feel of her tucked into his side. 'I was ten.'

'How long were you in there for?'

'About eighteen hours.'

Bella twisted slightly to look up at him, her eyes widening as she propped herself up on an elbow. 'Crikey. And you weren't missed?'

'Not for a while,' Will said flatly. 'I was supposed to be staying over with a friend.'

'So what happened?'

'We had an argument. I came home early.'

'And?'

He paused. Took a deep breath and steeled himself against the images he'd thought he'd buried in the depths of his memory, but were now flashing at the front of his brain in full, hideous colour. 'And I stumbled across something I shouldn't have.'

She went still at his side and her hand stopped meandering over his chest to come to a rest over his heart. 'What was it?'

He cleared his tight throat. 'My father. On the sofa. With my mother's best friend. And they weren't playing cards.'

Bella gasped softly. 'Oh, God.'

'Quite.'

'So you ran and hid,' she murmured.

'Wouldn't you?'

'I expect so. But didn't you yell or something?'

'Of course.' He summoned up a humourless smile. 'I guess they were too busy to hear me.'

'But what about the staff?'

'It was their afternoon off.'

She frowned. 'And your mother?'

'Here in London. Visiting friends.'

'So how did you get out?'

'The cleaner found me there the following morning.'

Bella's eyes filled with sympathy, her hand resumed

its wanderings and his chest contracted. 'How awful,' she breathed.

Well, yes, it had been, thought Will, but weirdly enough it didn't feel as awful right now as it used to.

'It wasn't the best afternoon I've ever had,' he muttered, slightly baffled by the fact that his brain seemed to be more interested in the feel of the woman lying beside him than the memories and ghosts that had haunted him for years. 'And it wasn't the last time my father was unfaithful to my mother,' he added, offloading a bit more and feeling something inside him lighten a little.

Caroline had been on to something, he thought, his mind briefly visiting the conversation he'd had with his aunt that afternoon in the bank. If he'd known unburdening himself would feel like this he'd have told someone years ago. It was seriously good to finally let the truth out. At least, some of it.

'So what did she do about it?'

A familiar twinge of guilt that he hadn't done more to help jabbed him in the stomach. 'Absolutely nothing. Just grinned and bore it. And suffered pretty much every minute of her life.'

Bella frowned. 'So why didn't she divorce him or something?'

Will sighed and rubbed a hand over his face. 'I told her to. On countless occasions. But unlike my father she believed in her vows.' He shrugged as if it couldn't matter less. 'And then she had a stroke and it was all over anyway.'

'I'm sorry,' she said softly and something in her voice made his chest squeeze.

'Yes, well, it was a long time ago.'

'Was that when you went to the Cayman Islands?'

He nodded briefly. 'And why. I had to get away.'

'Because you couldn't forgive him?'

And because he couldn't forgive himself. For any of it. 'Exactly,' he muttered thinking there were limits to what he was prepared to offload.

Bella blinked and stared at Will. Though she'd wanted him to open up to her, she hadn't expected any of this.

She hadn't expected to have her heartstrings tugged at the thought of a ten-year-old boy huddled in a cupboard, in all likelihood terrified and hungry and confused while his father got up close and personal with a family friend on the drawing-room sofa.

She hadn't expected to burn with anger at the selfishness of Will's father instead of lust.

And she hadn't expected to ache with compassion instead of desire.

But she was. And it was highly unsettling because she didn't want to be feeling any of this. To be honest, she'd assumed Will's aversion to commitment had had something to do with a failed relationship and if she'd known that probing was going to result in this kind of conversation she'd never have asked.

Not at all comfortable with the heart-wrenching emotions rolling around inside her, Bella determinedly pushed them to one side and focused on the bafflement that was battering her brain.

'But I thought your parents had the love affair of the century,' she said, lifting her eyes to his and feeling her heart squeeze at his rigid expression despite telling it not to.

'That's what everyone thinks. But the reality was actually something quite different. They weren't a one-off either,' Will added.

Huh? 'What on earth do you mean?' she said cautiously, not at all sure she wanted to know.

'It's a pack of lies, Bella,' he said. 'The whole damn lot of it. The men in my family are incapable of keeping their mar-

age vows much beyond the wedding night. Sometimes not
en until then.'

She opened her mouth. Then closed it as she struggled to
ocess the implications of what he was saying, but it was
most too great to comprehend. She didn't know where to
art. 'But the collection…?'

'Founded on the spoils of infidelity.'

'What?' She felt her eyes widen and her eyebrows shoot
). 'All of it?'

'Most of it.'

'I can't believe it,' she breathed, as one by one her illu-
ons of the Hawksley family's romantic affair with jewellery
ashed to the floor and shattered.

'Nevertheless, it's true. I'm sorry to disillusion you,' he
id gruffly.

And just like that Bella snapped herself out of it. Yes, to
arn that something she'd always admired and believed in
asn't true was something of a shock, but it paled into com-
arison when it came to what Will had gone through. A rib-
on of shame wound round her insides.

'You've been disillusioned too,' she said softly.

Will shrugged. 'I've had a long time to come to terms with
'

But had he? She thought about what his childhood must
ave been like. How much he must have suffered with no
blings to talk to and nowhere else to go. Just a great mau-
oleum of a house and two parents together, yet not, inside

Having kept it all bottled up inside, would he *ever* come
terms with it?

'No wonder you're so anti-commitment,' she murmured,
inking that in his situation she probably would be too. 'Isn't
lucky all I'm interested in is a casual fling?' she added with
lightness that she didn't really feel.

'Casual flings are all I ever have, Bella,' he said, his ex-

pression more serious than she'd ever seen it. 'And all I w
ever have.'

Bella felt a tiny shiver sprint down her spine. If that was
a warning she didn't know what was. And maybe that w
no bad thing. Maybe she'd needed a warning, because W
would be such an easy man to fall in love with.

Oh, she was immune, of course—she still had her lon
term goals at the forefront of her mind—but it wouldn't hu
to take a little extra care and remind herself to ignore tl
heart-tugging stuff and concentrate on the sex.

Speaking of which…

With ruthless determination Bella stamped down hard c
the disturbing emotions churning around inside her and f
cused on the way he could make her body feel instead. 'S
this minor thing you have a tiny problem with…'

Will relaxed a little and glanced at her. 'What about it?

'Don't you think twenty-six years is kind of a long tin
to be so completely held in its thrall?'

He propped himself up on an elbow and looked down
her. 'I hadn't really thought about it like that.'

'I'm kind of surprised you'd let it.'

'Yes, well, I've always believed that if something's wor
doing it's worth doing well.'

Bella grinned. 'Have you ever tried to get over it?'

'Frequently.'

'How?'

'The usual things.'

Her eyes widened. 'Therapy or hypnosis or something'
Somehow she really couldn't see it.

Will grimaced. 'Inner strength.'

Ah, that. She tilted her head, and injected a teasing gli
into her eye. 'Perhaps it's time you tried something else.'

'What do you suggest?'

'Perhaps me and the automatic locking mechanism of m

andcuffs will be able to think of something.' She sat up, dan-ling one from her finger and shooting him a saucy smile.

A muscle began to pound in his jaw. 'Perhaps,' he said, nd then reached out, plucked the handcuffs from her fingers, ressed her down and cuffed *her* to the bed.

Bella gasped as excitement whipped through her and set er nerve endings on fire. 'Oh, that's really not fair.'

Will's eyes blazed into hers and her heart raced. 'Having nticed me here under totally false pretences, I don't think ou're entitled to talk about fairness.'

'But I always knew I could release you,' she said breathily nd squirmed a little. 'How good are you with a hairpin?'

'Lousy.'

'So I could be here for some time?' And didn't that sound nore appealing than it ought to?

Will nodded and sat on the edge of the bed, his arms folded cross his chest as he looked slowly down the length of her ody. 'You could.'

Every inch of her burned and then began to melt. 'What bout your therapy?'

Will unclipped her stockings and slid them down her legs, o achingly slowly that Bella trembled. 'Later,' he murmured, unning the silk through his fingers and giving her a devas-atingly wicked smile before leaning forwards and wrapping he stockings over her eyes. 'Much later.'

CHAPTER THIRTEEN

IT WAS over.

The last of the guests had gone, the director of the mu
seum was locking up and Bella was standing alone in th
dark deserted alley, waiting for Will and summoning up th
strength to say goodbye. The exhibition had been a ragin
success and the collection was en route to Paris.

Whereas she, Bella thought wretchedly, was en route to
lifetime of misery.

She'd never imagined that the end of their affair would b
so excruciatingly painful. She'd never imagined that ever
fibre of her being could hurt, that her heart could physicall
ache. But it was. It was aching so much that it made her knee
tremble and her bones feel like rubber.

Because somewhere along the line, despite everything sh
knew about him, how pointless it was, she'd fallen in lov
with Will. Head-over-heels, stomach-flipping-with-every
smile in love with him.

Will was everything she'd ever wanted. And a whole lc
more. Over the last wonderful couple of weeks, they'd talked
laughed and had endless sex, and as she'd tumbled into lov
with him like a pebble in an avalanche she hadn't stood .
chance.

How could she ever have thought she'd be immune to him
she thought desolately. She had no defences whatsoever wher

e was concerned. They'd crumbled to dust long ago, leaving
er open and exposed and so very vulnerable.

Bella huddled into her coat as if that might somehow pro-
ect her from the pain as well as the cold.

Oh, she really shouldn't have come this evening. What had
he been thinking? When Will had invited her to the exhi-
ition's closing party earlier this afternoon she should have
aid no. She should have picked up her clothes, given him a
ool goodbye kiss and left with dignity.

But the thought of spending another couple of hours with
im before they separated for good had been too heart-
wrenchingly tempting to resist, and she'd given in, even
hough she'd known that she'd only be prolonging the agony.

Now the party was over and so was their affair.

As they'd agreed.

But did it really have to be?

Bella froze as the thought slammed into her head and her
heart began to thud with something that felt suspiciously like
hope. As it had done relentlessly over the last few days. And
hen she ruthlessly wiped it out because of course it had to
be over and she was an idiot to yearn for anything else.

She stamped her feet and watched Will come out of the
museum and walk towards her, aware that all they had left
were a few minutes and feeling her heart wobble.

He stood in front of her and she wrapped her arms around
her waist to stop herself reaching up and tracing his face with
her fingers in an effort to commit it to memory.

'So this is it,' she said, fixing an overly bright smile to her
ace to compensate for the crack in her voice.

Will looked down at her, his eyes guarded and expression
completely unreadable. 'I guess it is.'

'It's been…fun.'

He nodded. 'It has.'

A couple of seconds of silence fell and Bella's heart

twisted. This was awful. After all the time they'd spent to gether, everything they'd done, they'd been reduced to polit small talk as if they were awkward strangers. 'Will I see yo at Alex and Phoebe's wedding?' she said.

'It's unlikely. I'm flying home tomorrow. I don't know when I'll be back.'

'Right.' She frowned and bit her lip and focused her gaz on the banner bearing the museum's name that hung from flagpole and fluttered in the breeze.

'I hope you find what you're looking for, Bella,' he mur mured and she could feel his gaze roaming over her face.

Her vision blurred and she blinked to clear it, her whol body clenching in agony. Because she'd already found it hadn't she? 'You too.'

He reached out and ran a finger down her cheek and sh trembled. And then he was pulling her against him, wrap ping his arms around her and crushing his mouth to hers.

With her heart banging crazily against her ribs, Bella clutched at his shirt, melted into him and completely lost her self in the kiss that was hot and devastating and, she had the sensation, filled with everything that he couldn't, or wouldn't say.

But even as that last thought spun through her head Wil was drawing back and unwinding himself from her. Withou another word he turned on his heel and strode off, head dow with his hands thrust deep in his pockets.

Bella stood there, her heart thumping, her stomach churn ing and her body on fire as she watched him march out of he life.

Her head pounded as questions and hopes and dreams began to bombard her on all sides. Was she really going to leave it like this? To be haunted by that kiss and what it migh have meant? Never knowing how Will really felt about her' Never knowing if things might have changed for him, the way they had for her? Never knowing if he was holding back because of what he thought she wanted?

She couldn't. She had to see… She had to take a chance…

With her blood roaring in her ears, Bella took a deep breath and ran after him. 'Will, wait.'

Will barely broke his stride.

'Wait,' she yelled again, and then he gradually slowed, stopped and turned to face her.

'What?' he said, his voice sounding strained and hoarse and his face set.

Light from the street lamp cast shadows across the planes of his face and her heart clutched with longing. Bella swallowed and looked up at him, knowing that her eyes were shimmering with hope but unable to wipe it out. 'Does this really have to be the end?'

Will's jaw was tight, but his eyes burned. 'You know it does.'

'Why?'

'Because it's for the best.'

Bella took a deep breath. She didn't want platitudes. She wanted honesty, even if he didn't. 'I'm not so sure it is.'

He frowned, shook his head faintly as if warning her not to do this, that pursuing this would only lead to heartbreak. *Her* heartbreak. But now she'd started she couldn't stop, whatever the probable outcome.

'The thing is,' she said, lifting her chin, her blood pounding in her ears as she put her heart in his hands, 'I've fallen in love with you.'

For a moment there was silence. Will blinked. Paled a fraction beneath his tan. 'I see.'

His voice was totally devoid of emotion and Bella felt as if she'd been punched in the stomach. 'Is that all you have to say?'

'What else is there?'

She took a deep breath to silence the voice in her head yelling at her to stop. To save herself from more unfathomable anguish. 'How about telling me that you love me too?'

He froze, and she could see great barriers springing up all round him. 'I can't do that.'

'Why not?' she said, her voice cracking.

'I just can't.'

And never would.

The words remained unspoken, but Bella could see it in his eyes and the pain that scythed through her nearly floored her. Her heart lay crushed and bleeding in his hands and to her horror her throat closed over and tears pricked the backs of her eyes.

She gulped. Fought for dignity as she wondered how he had the power to do this to her. How he could willingly and cold-bloodedly do this to her, because he must know he was destroying her, mustn't he?

As that knowledge tortured her something inside her leapt up and obliterated her self-control.

'You know what?' she said, all the frustration and pain and crushing disappointment hurtling around her in a great mighty seething mass. 'This aversion to commitment you have is crap.'

Will recoiled as if she'd slapped him in the face. 'What?'

'Being alone isn't good,' she said, her eyes flashing and her body shaking as she took a step closer and jabbed him in the chest. 'Being alone isn't clever.'

'Nevertheless it's my only option,' he snapped.

'But why?'

'Betrayal is in my genes.' His voice was tight.

Her eyebrows shot up as she stared at him. 'Do you really believe that?'

'How can I believe anything else?'

She gaped at him, for a moment too stunned to know how

to respond. And then she really saw red. She didn't care that they were standing in a cold dark cobbled street. She didn't care who heard them. As long as he did. 'What complete and utter rubbish,' she said. 'If genetics ruled, I'd have followed my mother into a life of crime instead of establishing a successful totally legitimate business.'

'Well, maybe you're more like your father, whoever he was.'

'And maybe you're not,' she fired back.

The vibrating silence stretched between them. 'Who do you resemble, Will?' she said eventually.

He threw her a furious scowl. 'That's irrelevant.'

As she thought. 'You know this is absolutely insane. You aren't only your father's son. You're your mother's too. So why should his genes outweigh hers?'

For a long moment Will didn't say anything, but his face was tight. And then something inside him seemed to collapse. His shoulders fell, the anger faded from his expression and his eyes filled with something that made her heart clench. 'It really doesn't matter,' he said hoarsely. 'I'm not willing to take the risk.'

'What risk?'

'That I might hurt you.'

But couldn't he see that he was hurting her right now? That he was pulling her heart apart piece by tiny piece? She wanted to thump him on the chest, claw at his skin and hurt him as much as he was hurting her.

'You are not your father, Will, and I am not your mother. God, I'm not even my mother.' She threw her hands up and let out a short bitter laugh. 'I can't believe you're letting this still dictate your life. Just because your ancestors were unfaithful it doesn't automatically follow that you will be too.'

'Doesn't it?' he grated, his eyes glittering.

'Of course not. God,' she said, summoning up her anger

to block out the hurt. 'You're one of the most intelligent people I've ever met so why are you being so pig-headed about
this?'

'Because I was,' he practically roared, the words sounding as if they'd been torn from somewhere deep, deep inside
him.

Bella froze. Her eyebrows shot up and her mouth dropped.
'What?'

Will sighed, took a step back and raked his hands through
his hair. 'I *was* unfaithful, Bella. Only once. But it was
enough.'

Bella stared at him in complete shock. 'When?'

'Years ago. When I was twenty-three.'

'But why? What happened?'

He twisted away from her. 'I don't really want to talk about
it.'

'Well, that's tough,' she said, moving back into his line of
vision. 'Because I do. I've just told you I love you. The very
least you can give me is an explanation as to why you can't
do the same.'

'There isn't a lot to explain.'

'Then it shouldn't take long.'

'Fine,' he said through gritted teeth. 'I had a girlfriend. I
was unfaithful to her. End of story.'

Definitely not the end of the story. 'Why?'

He glanced at her and frowned. 'What difference does that
make?'

'It makes all the difference in the world, because I don't
believe you'd sleep with someone else for the sake of it.'
Despite currently behaving like a stubborn idiot, he had far
too much integrity. If he had been unfaithful then there must
have been a very good reason for it.

Will shoved his hands through his hair. 'Tania and I went
out for around six months. She was bipolar. Not that either of

us knew then. In my naivety I thought she had one of those extreme personalities. When she was on a high it was thrilling and I was only too happy to go along for the ride.' He shrugged. 'But then she started behaving strangely. Going off on her own and drinking more. For a while I thought it might have had something to do with me.'

He gave her a melancholic little smile and her heart twanged. 'It couldn't have been you.'

'I know. At the time, though, I didn't know what to believe. My mother had just died and my father started being difficult, not that that's any excuse. Anyway, the depression spiralled out of control so swiftly… I guess I didn't know how to cope. I just sort of unravelled.'

Bella's throat stung. 'You were young.'

Will sighed and rubbed a hand over his face. 'Not that young. I should have been able to handle it. Instead, after one particularly harrowing weekend I went to a bar, drank myself into oblivion and woke up in a stranger's bed.'

And he was still riddled with guilt. It was in his eyes and in his expression. 'What happened after that?'

'I immediately went round to her flat and confessed everything.'

'And?'

'We split up. She moved in with her parents and I went to the Cayman Islands.'

'Did you ever see her again?'

Will nodded. 'A couple of years later we met up for a drink when I was here for a conference. We talked. She'd got a lot better and told me she didn't blame me. That she'd have probably done the same if the roles had been reversed.'

Bella tilted her head and wished there were something she could say to take away the guilt and the torment filling his eyes. 'Everyone makes mistakes, Will. Especially when they're young.'

'Yes, but not quite like the one I made.'

She tilted her head. 'Well, no. But you don't seriously think you'd do it again, do you?'

His expression turned bleak. 'It's not a risk I'm prepared to take.'

Bella's heart wobbled as the world seemed to stop turning for a moment. 'Ever?'

'Ever.'

'Then I feel sorry for you. Because based on a very specific set of circumstances that took place years ago you're depriving yourself of the chance to find true happiness. And that's a tragedy.'

His jaw was set, his expression implacable. 'How can you say that with such certainty? How can you can believe in love and faith and happily ever after when you've never had it?'

'Because I'm an optimist. Because I know it's out there and I've seen it. And because *I* don't let my past rule my life. *I* don't run and hide when my demons leap in front of me.'

Will shrugged and his eyes went bleak. 'Then you're stronger than I am.'

That was ridiculous. She'd never seen strength like his and to see him not want to fight for them was agonising. 'She forgave you, Will,' Bella said, silently pleading with him to give them a chance. 'Why can't you forgive yourself?'

'I just can't.'

And with those three words all her hopes and dreams crashed to the ground, smashing into smithereens at her feet while her heart splintered into a million pieces. 'I see,' she said, somehow managing to pull her shoulders back and give him a shaky smile because she couldn't let herself fall apart in front of him. 'So this really is it.'

He nodded. 'It really is.'

CHAPTER FOURTEEN

Of all the ways to spend a Saturday, attending a wedding when she was feeling so miserable and wretched wouldn't have been her number one choice, thought Bella bleakly, staring at the flowers at the front of the church and swallowing back the ball of misery that seemed to be lodged in her throat pretty much permanently these days.

She really hadn't wanted to come. Not when she was feeling so listless, so lacking in energy and sparkle and so damn sad.

But Phoebe, who'd prised the whole sorry story out of her over a bottle of wine one evening—thankfully managing to refrain from battering her with a string of 'told you so's—had begged her to think about it, and in the end she'd refused to let her wretchedness spill over onto her friend's happiness.

So she'd hauled on a suitable outfit, slapped on several gallons of anti-puffiness eye cream and an entire tubeful of highlighter, and here she was. Sitting several pews back from the altar, next to one of the many single eligible men Phoebe had told her were in attendance, and trying to focus on the colourful array of hats instead of the ache in her heart.

At least there wasn't any danger of bumping into Will, she thought dully. Phoebe had told her that he'd sent an email from the Cayman Islands saying he wouldn't be able to make it, and Bella had managed to convince herself that this was a huge relief.

How she'd got through the last fortnight she'd never know. At first, like a fool, she'd envisaged scenarios in which Will came to his senses, pitched up on her doorstep, told her he'd been an idiot and swept her into his arms. Because she'd been so sure he loved her, so sure that they'd connected in a way that went far deeper than sex.

But how wrong she'd been. He hadn't pitched up on her doorstep and swept her into his arms, and as the days had passed she'd sunk further and further into despair. Work had been impossible and wafting around her flat, every inch of which held one memory of Will or another, had been agonising.

Eventually, unable to stand London and moping around it any longer, Bella had gone to stay with her mother. After a couple of days, however, the goats and the homoeopathic advice had got too much and she'd come back because no amount of arnica could heal her battered soul.

It was so frustrating, she thought as her heart squeezed and her vision blurred. She *knew* she and Will could have been happy together if only he'd given them a chance. Why couldn't he see that nothing in life was guaranteed? That nothing was certain. That all that anyone could hope for was to have love and respect and trust, and hope that that was enough.

She really didn't want to have to come to terms with the fact that Will, the stubborn jerk, might be too damaged by what he'd done to ever let himself get close to anyone ever again. But what alternative did she have?

The image of his face, his smile, the light in his eyes when he shot her a glance, floated into her head and her throat tightened. She hiccuped and stared determinedly at the ceiling. At least here if she burst into tears, as she was prone to do at he drop of a hat, everyone would think she was overcome with emotion at the happiness of the occasion.

With any luck, she told herself as the organ struck up and she got to her feet, within an hour or so her emotions would be overcome with champagne.

What in God's name was he doing here? Will wondered for the millionth time, shifting on the pew at the back of the church and running a finger around the inside of his collar. He was supposed to be at home. Five thousand miles away. Working. Or at least trying to. At the very least he was supposed to be staying away and giving Bella the chance to get over him, the way he was getting over her.

So what had made him leap up from his desk at three o'clock yesterday afternoon and tell his team that they'd be holding the fort for the next few days? What had made him pay a fortune for a last minute plane ticket to London, grab his morning suit and instruct his butler to prepare the house for him? And what had made him take a trip to Bond Street the second he'd landed?

It was so rash, so out of character, that it scared the hell out of him. But then he couldn't remember the last time that his behaviour had been *in* character.

Nor could he remember a time when Bella wasn't in his head.

Getting over her? Ha. That was a joke. So much for telling himself as he watched her walk away the evening they'd parted that the memory of her would fade. So much for convincing himself he'd done the right thing. That he'd been protecting them both.

The anguish in her eyes and on her face when he'd told her that he wouldn't ever risk loving her had been haunting his dreams. The accusations she'd flung at him had been battering away at his brain constantly until he'd been forced to acknowledge that walking away might not have been the right thing to do at all.

Bella, on the other hand, had been right about everything. How could he ever have thought that there was nothing special about her? How could he ever have convinced himself that he'd have spilled his guts about his parents and the truth about the collection to anyone? How could he have been so blind? How could he have rejected everything she'd offered?

God, he was sick of running and hiding. He was sick of being alone and tired of the endless guilt. Didn't he deserve a stab at happiness? Didn't Bella? Didn't everyone?

Look at Alex, standing at the altar looking down at Phoebe as if they were the only two people in the church, and saying the vows that Will had always been so sceptical about. There was no way Alex could be certain that what he had with Phoebe was going to last. No way he could know that he wasn't going to let her down ever.

But maybe that was the point, Will thought, the blood pumping around his veins a fraction faster than normal as all the random strands of thinking he'd unwillingly done over the course of the last few weeks merged into one.

Maybe no one could ever know anything for certain. Maybe if you loved someone enough, if you'd found everything you'd ever wanted in that one person, you just had to take a leap of faith. Maybe if you believed in yourselves and each other, you could get through anything.

He rubbed his chest as his stomach churned and his head pounded and all the hopes and dreams he'd managed to bury for years sprang to life. His pulse began to thunder as the possibilities opened up before him and for the first time in his life he caught a glimpse of what he could have if only he gave himself a break.

'Are you all right?'

Will blinked and turned to the elderly lady on his left.

'I'm not sure,' he murmured. He didn't think he'd been all right for quite a while.

She brought out a flask from beneath her coat and offered it to him. 'Brandy. Have some.'

'No, thanks,' he said, with the hint of a smile. He didn't need brandy. He didn't need anything. Except Bella. God, how he needed her.

But was it really that simple? Would Bella ever forgive him for being such a stubborn, selfish fool? Or had she got over him and moved on days ago?

Blind panic speared through him at the thought that he might have screwed everything up for good and his whole body went cold. And then he forced himself to calm down, because that was not an option. In fact the sooner he sorted this out, the better, he thought firmly, scouring the congregation for her and desperately hoping he hadn't left it too late.

And then he saw her. Sitting on the other side of the church looking wan but gorgeous and staring at the ceiling and Will realised with a blinding flash of clarity that it was that simple and he knew exactly why he'd come.

He'd deliberately blown one chance of happiness. He didn't intend blowing another.

Bella clutched at her glass of champagne and wished it were a bucket to which she had the only straw. Her face ached with the effort of maintaining the rictus grin she'd been wearing for the last half an hour, and she wasn't sure she could manage much more in the way of chat. She congratulated the bride and groom, who looked so happy that it made her heart bleed with both delight and, she was ashamed to admit, envy, and that was the main thing. Now she could drink herself into oblivion without having to worry about sounding sensible.

She took another sip of her second—or was it third?—

glass of champagne and tuned out of the conversation rattling around her.

Maybe she'd get a cat. A cat didn't have problems with trust and obstinacy and forgiveness, did it? No, you knew where you were with a cat. They were simple creatures. Unlike men. Unlike Will…

Bella's heart lurched and she squeezed her eyes tight shut against the images that flickered through her head. Damn. There he was again. Invading her head, the way he did all the damn time.

Well, she was sick of it. Utterly sick of it. She'd had two weeks of feeling like this and she was fed up with it. She'd had enough of the constant misery, the agonising pain that relentlessly gnawed away at her and the hopeless sense of despair that accompanied her everywhere she went.

Why should she be doomed to a life of singledom just because of Will's emotional cowardice? She glanced around and took another sip of champagne. *How* many single eligible men had Phoebe said there were here this evening? A dozen? Two dozen? Surely one of them would be a fan of commitment and relatively baggage free.

So she'd chat and flirt and have fun for a change. Maybe even throw herself on the dance floor later and shake her groove.

Oh, yes, she thought, holding out her glass to be refilled by a hovering waiter. She was going to get over Will, come hell or high water. Because what option did she have? Was she going to spend the rest of her life pining after him? No, she was not.

One thing was for sure though. She was done with emotion. Emotion made you unstable and unpredictable, and only led to heartbreak. So from now on she was going to be practical. Ruthless. She'd take no prisoners. Break some balls. She was going to—

'Bella.'

At the sound of the voice behind her Bella froze and whatever she'd thought she'd been going to do went clean out of her head. All her blood rushed to her feet and she swayed. Her stomach leapt, her heart lurched and the room swam. Oh, no. Please, no. Not again.

She closed her eyes and tried not to panic. Maybe she'd imagined Will's voice. Maybe to add insult to injury she'd finally lost her mind. Because he was supposed to be on the other side of the planet, wasn't he? Conquering the day-trading world or whatever it was he did and cowering behind his hang-ups.

But while her imagination had been pretty active recently, it wasn't so good that it could conjure up the intoxicating scent of him. Or the heat of his body. Or the familiar instant response of *her* body.

Slowly she turned, her heart beating so hard she feared it might leap out of her chest, and thought frantically about how she was going to handle this.

'Oh, Will, hi,' she said brightly, deciding that 'greeting an old friend' and acting as if his appearance at the wedding didn't mean a thing to her was the way forward.

'Hi,' he said, his eyes dark and unfathomable and fixed unwaveringly on hers.

Bella held herself still, which was hard when every cell in her body longed to fling itself at him. It had only been a couple of weeks since she'd last seen him but it felt like a century and despite everything it was so heavenly to see him. Even though he looked haggard and exhausted.

Ignoring the urge to stroke the weariness from his face, Bella injected some much-needed steel into her spine. 'I didn't think you were planning to be here.'

'I wasn't.'

A tiny spark of hope rushed through her at the thought

he'd come to see her and she stamped it out. Ruthlessly, of course, because she was done with emotion, wasn't she? She twisted the glass in her hands and then made herself stop it. 'So how are the Cayman Islands?'

'Still there.'

'And work?'

'Fine.'

'How nice.'

'I'm thinking of transferring my business back here.'

Bella's heart leapt. 'Oh?' she said, unable this time to obliterate the hope that his decision might have something to do with her.

Will nodded. 'Running the dukedom from so far away is proving tricky.'

Her heart sank and she wished she could kick herself. See? This was why she had to be practical instead of emotional. Emotional simply hurt too much. 'I can imagine.'

He stared at her and for some reason her heart began to thunder despite her attempts to tell it not to. 'Although it's not just that.'

'No?' Her mouth went dry.

'No.'

So what else was it? she desperately wanted to know. But he didn't elaborate and no way was she going to ask.

'Great wedding, don't you think?' He gave her a faint smile and she felt like kicking him, because he must know he was rubbing a ton of salt into a raw open wound.

'The best,' she said, furious with the way he could still make her feel. 'A top London hotel, fabulous food and drink and a twenty piece swing band. What could be better?'

'They look happy,' he added, looking over to where Alex and Phoebe were gazing adoringly into each other's eyes.

'They are.' And then anger and frustration surged through her. Because what was all this about? Did he have *any* idea of he distress he was causing her by just being here? 'So why did you come, Will? I didn't think you did weddings.'

Will rubbed a hand along his jaw and shrugged, as if it was a mystery to him as well. 'Neither did I. Now I do, we need to talk.'

What for? So he could tell her again how he couldn't risk a relationship with her? No way. 'No, we don't.'

'We do. Because you have no idea of how so sorry I am about the way our affair ended.'

She shrugged as if she'd forgotten all about it and ignored the knives making mincemeat of her heart. 'Don't be. Really, it's nothing. I've moved on.' She waved at the man she'd been sitting next to in the church and shot him a bright smile.

Will frowned as he looked in the direction she was waving in and went still. 'Have you?'

'Oh, yes, absolutely,' she said, nodding and smiling like a lunatic.

She swung her gaze back to him and saw that he'd gone a little pale. 'And have you found what you're looking for?'

'I'm getting there,' she said breezily, reminding herself it didn't matter what colour he went.

He shoved his hands in his pockets, the muscle in his jaw hammering as his eyes blazed into hers. 'So I don't suppose there's any point in asking you to marry me.'

'Absolutely none whatso—' Bella stopped. Blinked. The blood roared in her ears and for a moment she thought she might be about to pass out. God, how many glasses of champagne had she had? 'What?' she croaked.

Will took her arm and Bella let herself be pulled behind an enormous flower arrangement, too stunned to resist. 'I said, I don't suppose there's any point in asking you to marry me.'

She jerked her gaze to his and scoured his expression, but found nothing to indicate that he was anything other than completely serious. 'That's what I thought you said.'

The pulse at the base of his neck was hammering. 'Good So what do you think?'

What did she think? *What did she think?* Bella blinked and thought that she didn't have a clue what she thought about anything any more. Because shouldn't she be ecstatic? Shouldn't she be leaping around with joy and delight and happiness? She was being offered everything she'd ever wanted by the man she loved to distraction.

So why wasn't she jumping into his arms and smothering him in kisses? Why couldn't she forget the way they'd parted? The flat bleak way he'd looked at her as he told her he'd never let himself love her? Or the fact that he must have known what he was doing to her but had carried on regardless?

Did he really expect her to forget the way he'd hurt her and simply tumble gratefully into his arms as if he was the answer to all her prayers? If he thought that he could think again.

Will watched the emotions play across Bella's face, his heart racing and a bead of sweat trickling down his spine. This wasn't going the way he'd imagined. He hadn't had the time to think it through in great depth, but he'd rather assumed that he'd propose and she'd fling herself into his arms, smile up at him as she pressed herself up close and say yes in that gorgeous breathy way she had. And then they'd go and set about making each other deliriously happy for the rest of their lives.

So what was she doing standing there stock still with a frown creasing her forehead and a wary look in her eye?

'But you don't want to marry anyone,' she said carefully and something in his stomach curdled. 'You don't do commitment. You have issues.'

Will went cold at the flat tone of her voice. 'I know. But I'm working on them.'

'You said you'd never take the risk on us. You said you ouldn't.'

'I know,' he muttered again, the panic flooding back as it lawned on him that he was staggering around on unknown erritory in the dark without a torch.

'Do you have *any* idea how much that hurt?'

Her eyes flashed with pain, the pain that *he'd* caused. 'I'm orry,' he said, his throat as rough and dry as sandpaper. 'I'd lo anything to be able to go back and fix things.'

She tilted her head and shrugged as if she couldn't care ess. 'So what's changed?' she asked, arching an eyebrow and hooting him a cool glance, and for the first time in his life Vill knew what real fear felt like.

It felt like an icy hand clutching his heart. It felt like a gallon of acid swilling around in his stomach. It felt like the pleakness of a lifetime of loneliness, a future that yawned thead of him empty and cold.

'I have,' he said, clearing his throat in an effort to beat back he bone-chilling dread that he'd screwed things up beyond epair.

'I see.'

And as he looked at her, clearly deliberating over what lecision she was going to make, he realised he was going to nave to fight as he'd never had to fight before.

'I'm sorry I reacted like a jerk when you told me you loved ne,' he said, nearly passing out with the force with which ev-erything he wanted to say slammed into his head. 'I'm sorry couldn't tell you I loved you. I didn't think I deserved it. never allowed myself to wish for it. I didn't think I could nave it.'

Bella blinked. 'You could have had everything,' she aid simply, and his heart wrenched. 'And you rejected it. Deliberately.'

'I was terrified.'

Her eyes widened. 'Terrified?'

Will raked his hands through his hair and dragged in a deep ragged breath. 'My feelings for you scared the hell out of me. They still do a bit, to be honest.'

Bella frowned. 'And what feelings would those be?' she said cautiously.

'I have so many I barely know where to start.'

'Well, I'm not going anywhere,' she said, her frown disappearing as she flashed him the ghost of a smile. A smile that, however faint, warmed his soul and gave him more encouragement than he could have hoped for.

Will swallowed and felt a tremor run through him. 'I am utterly in awe of you, Bella. The way you don't let the past dictate your future. The way you've always chosen the path you want to take. The way you face your demons head-on and don't hide behind anything. You are the bravest, most incredible woman I've ever met.'

A light flickered in the depths of her eyes and his heart began to thunder. 'Really?'

He nodded. 'Really. You are also beautiful and clever and kind and talented and-'

Her smile deepened. 'Don't forget my wicked way with a pair of handcuffs.'

'As if I could ever forget that.' He gazed at her. 'I love you, Bella. I love you more than I ever thought possible and I just want to do everything in my power to make you happy. To make your dreams come true.' He paused. Felt his heart quake a little. 'If you'll let me, that is.'

As if she'd ever really had any choice, thought Bella, her whole body shaking with happiness as she looked up at the earnest expression on his face and the promise blazing in his eyes. She'd been utterly lost the minute he'd admitted to being terrified. Ah, who was she kidding? She'd been lost the minute she'd laid eyes on him.

'That was quite a speech,' she said, feeling an unstoppable smile spread across her face.

Will frowned. 'Yes, well, I've no doubt it could have been better but I didn't have much of a chance to practise.'

'You didn't need to,' she said, closing the distance between them and winding her arms around his neck. 'It was perfect.'

Letting out a deep breath, and with it all the tension that had been gripping his body, Will folded his arms around her and clasped her against him as if he never wanted to let her go. 'You can't imagine how delighted I am you think so.' His eyes blazed into hers and Bella trembled. 'So will you? Let me try and give you everything you want, I mean.'

'I think I probably should.' She lifted her eyebrows and grinned up at him. 'After all, it sounds like you could learn a lot from me.'

'I could.'

And then he lowered his head and captured her mouth with his and kissed her with the passion of everything he'd just said. He kissed her until she was melting with desire and happiness and love.

'Not to mention the fact that I love you too,' she murmured against his mouth.

He bent back a little and smiled. 'Despite my many failings?'

'And because of them.' She grinned. 'And I'm not exactly without fault, you know.'

'You are to me.'

She traced the creases at his eyes with her fingertips and felt him shake. 'You look like hell.'

'The last couple of weeks haven't exactly been my finest.'

'Nor mine.'

'You look amazing. You smell amazing.' He rested his forehead against hers and closed his eyes. 'God, I'm sorry I was such an idiot. And for so long.'

'That's OK. You can spend the rest of your life making it up to me.'

'I intend to.' Then he released her, dug in his pocket and drew out a small velvet box and handed it to her. 'This is for you.'

Bella took the box with shaking fingers, her heart squeezing and her throat tightening.

'Actually, maybe you shouldn't open it now,' he said, his voice sounding a little shaky. 'Maybe you should open it later. Maybe doing this kind of thing at someone else's wedding isn't really all that appropriate.'

'Nervous, Will?' she said with a tiny smile.

'Petrified. I've never bought jewellery before. Plus, you're a jeweller and that makes the whole thing even more nerve-racking.'

Holding her breath, Bella released the catch and slowly opened the box. And there, nestling in a bed of deep purple velvet, was the most beautiful diamond solitaire ring she'd ever seen.

'Do you like it?' he said.

Like it? Her breathing was all over the place and her eyes were stinging, because it was everything she'd ever imagined, everything she'd ever hoped for, and so much more. 'It's beautiful. I love it. And I love you.'

'Then please say you'll marry me,' he said softly, taking the box from her and sliding the ring onto her finger.

She stared up at him, saw the love blazing in his eyes and wondered if it was possible to be happier. She gave him a dazzling smile and wrapped her arms around his neck, pressed herself against him and breathed, 'Well, if you absolutely insist…'

* * * * *

CLASSIC

Harlequin *Presents*

EXTRA

You can find more information on upcoming Harlequin®
titles, free excerpts and more at www.Harlequin.com.

HPECNM0512

REQUEST YOUR FREE BOOKS!

Harlequin *Presents*

PASSION GUARANTEED SEDUCTION

2 FREE NOVELS PLUS
2 FREE GIFTS!

YES! Please send me 2 FREE Harlequin Presents® novels and my 2 FREE gifts (gifts are worth about $10). After receiving them, if I don't wish to receive any more books, I can return the shipping statement marked "cancel." If I don't cancel, I will receive 6 brand-new novels every month and be billed just $4.30 per book in the U.S. or $4.99 per book in Canada. That's a saving of at least 14% off the cover price! It's quite a bargain! Shipping and handling is just 50¢ per book in the U.S. and 75¢ per book in Canada.* I understand that accepting the 2 free books and gifts places me under no obligation to buy anything. I can always return a shipment and cancel at any time. Even if I never buy another book, the two free books and gifts are mine to keep forever.

106/306 HDN FERQ

Name	(PLEASE PRINT)
Address	Apt. #
City	State/Prov. Zip/Postal Code
Signature (if under 18, a parent or guardian must sign)	

Mail to the **Reader Service:**
IN U.S.A.: P.O. Box 1867, Buffalo, NY 14240-1867
IN CANADA: P.O. Box 609, Fort Erie, Ontario L2A 5X3

Not valid for current subscribers to Harlequin Presents books.

**Are you a current subscriber to Harlequin Presents books
and want to receive the larger-print edition?
Call 1-800-873-8635 or visit www.ReaderService.com.**

* Terms and prices subject to change without notice. Prices do not include applicable taxes. Sales tax applicable in N.Y. Canadian residents will be charged applicable taxes. Offer not valid in Quebec. This offer is limited to one order per household. All orders subject to credit approval. Credit or debit balances in a customer's account(s) may be offset by any other outstanding balance owed by or to the customer. Please allow 4 to 6 weeks for delivery. Offer available while quantities last.

Your Privacy—The Reader Service is committed to protecting your privacy. Our Privacy Policy is available online at www.ReaderService.com or upon request from the Reader Service.

We make a portion of our mailing list available to reputable third parties that offer products we believe may interest you. If you prefer that we not exchange your name with third parties, or if you wish to clarify or modify your communication preferences, please visit us at www.ReaderService.com/consumerschoice or write to us at Reader Service Preference Service, P.O. Box 9062, Buffalo, NY 14269. Include your complete name and address.

Harlequin® *Romance*

A touching new duet from fan-favorite author

SUSAN MEIER

When millionaire CEO Max Montgomery spots
Kate Hunter-Montgomery—the wife he's never forgotten—
back in town with a daughter who looks just like him, he's
determined to win her back. But can this savvy business tycoon
convince Kate to trust him a second time with her heart?

Find out this June in

THE TYCOON'S SECRET DAUGHTER

And look for book 2 coming this August!

NANNY FOR THE MILLIONAIRE'S TWINS

www.Harlequin.com

HR17811

*The legacy of the powerful
Sicilian Ferrara dynasty continues in
THE FORBIDDEN FERRARA
by* USA TODAY *bestselling author Sarah Morgan.*

Enjoy this sneak peek!

A Ferrara would never sit down at a Baracchi table for fear of being poisoned.

Fia had no idea why Santo was here. He didn't know.

He *couldn't* know.

"*Buona sera,* Fia."

A deep male voice came from the doorway, and she turned. The crazy thing was, she didn't know his voice. But she knew his eyes and they were looking at her now—two dark pools of dangerous black. They gleamed bright with intelligence and hard with ruthless purpose. They were the eyes of a man who thrived in a cutthroat business environment. A man who knew what he wanted and wasn't afraid to go after it. They were the same eyes that had glittered into hers in the darkness three years before as they'd ripped each other's clothes and slaked a fierce hunger.

He was exactly the same. Still the same "born to rule" Ferrara self-confidence; the same innate sophistication, polished until it shone bright as the paintwork of his Lamborghini.

She wanted him to go to hell and stay there.

He was her biggest mistake.

And judging from the cold, cynical glint in his eye, he considered her to be his.

"Well, this is a surprise. The Ferrara brothers don't usually step down from their ivory tower to mingle with us mortals. Checking out the competition?" She adopted her most businesslike tone, while all the time her anxiety was rising and the questions were pounding through her head.

Did he know?

Had he found out?

A faint smile touched his mouth and the movement distracted her. There was an almost deadly beauty in the sensual curve of those lips. Everything about the man was dark and sexual, as if he'd been designed for the express purpose of drawing women to their doom. If rumor were correct, he did that with appalling frequency.

Fia wasn't fooled by his apparently relaxed pose or his deceptively mild tone.

Santo Ferrara was the most dangerous man she'd ever met.

Will Santo discover Fia's secret?

Find out in THE FORBIDDEN FERRARA
by USA TODAY bestselling author Sarah Morgan,
available this June from Harlequin Presents®!

EXP0612